Joyce
Marx
Hardy
Machiavelli
Chesterton
Cooper
Emerson
Austen
Abbott
Defoe
Montaigne
Hugo
Grimm
Melville
Eliot
Haggard
Stoker
Molière
Christie
Carroll
Wilde
Byron
Maupassant
Engels
Schiller
Garnett
Fitzgerald
Hawthorne
Smith
Kafka
Goethe
Einstein
Dostoyevsky
Hall
Cotton
Kipling
Doyle
Willis
Baum
Henry
Nietzsche
Leslie
Dumas
Flaubert
Turgenev
Balzac
Stockton
Vatsyayana
Crane
Burroughs
Verne
Curtis
Tocqueville
Gogol
Vinci
Homer
Widger
Tolstoy
Whitman
Busch
Darwin
Thoreau
Potter
Freud
Zola
Twain
Plato
Scott Harte
Kant
Jowett
Stevenson
Dickens
Hesse
Burton
Andersen
London
Descartes
Cervantes
Voltaire
Poe
Aristotle
Wells
Cooke
Hale
James
Hastings
Bunner
Shakespeare
Irving
Richter
Chambers
da
Shaw
Doré
Dante
Chekhov
Wodehouse
Benedict
Alcott
Swift
Pushkin
Newton

Monsieur Maurice

Amelia Ann Blanford Edwards

Imprint

This book is part of TREDITION CLASSICS

Author: Amelia Ann Blanford Edwards
Cover design: Buchgut, Berlin – Germany

Publisher: tredition GmbH, Hamburg - Germany
ISBN: 978-3-8424-3338-0

www.tredition.com
www.tredition.de

Copyright:
The content of this book is sourced from the public domain.

The intention of the TREDITION CLASSICS series is to make world literature in the public domain available in printed format. Literary enthusiasts and organizations, such as Project Gutenberg, world-wide have scanned and digitally edited the original texts. tredition has subsequently formatted and redesigned the content into a modern reading layout. Therefore, we cannot guarantee the exact reproduction of the original format of a particular historic edition. Please also note that no modifications have been made to the spelling, therefore it may differ from the orthography used today.

MONSIEUR MAURICE

By

AMELIA B. EDWARDS

1873

1

The events I am about to relate took place more than fifty years ago. I am a white-haired old woman now, and I was then a little girl scarce ten years of age; but those times, and the places and people associated with them, seem, in truth, to lie nearer my memory than the times and people of to-day. Trivial incidents which, if they had happened yesterday, would be forgotten, come back upon me sometimes with all the vivid detail of a photograph; and words unheeded many a year ago start out, like the handwriting on the wall, in sudden characters of fire.

But this is no new experience. As age creeps on, we all have the same tale to tell. The days of our youth are those we remember best and most fondly, and even the sorrows of that bygone time become pleasures in the retrospect. Of my own solitary childhood I retain the keenest recollection, as the following pages will show.

My father's name was Bernhard—Johann Ludwig Bernhard; and he was a native of Coblentz on the Rhine. Having grown grey in the Prussian service, fought his way slowly and laboriously from the ranks upward, been seven times wounded and twice promoted on the field, he was made colonel of his regiment in 1814, when the Allies entered Paris. In 1819, being no longer fit for active service, he retired on a pension, and was appointed King's steward of the Château of Augustenburg at Brühl—a sort of military curatorship to which few duties and certain contingent emoluments were attached. Of these last, a suite of rooms in the Château, a couple of acres of private garden, and the revenue accruing from a small local impost, formed the most important part. It was towards the latter half of this year (1819) that, having now for the first time in his life a settled home in which to receive me, my father fetched me from Nuremberg where I was living with my aunt, Martha Baur, and took me to reside with him at Brühl.

Now my aunt, Martha Baur, was an exemplary person in her way; a rigid Lutheran, a strict disciplinarian, and the widow of a wealthy wool-stapler. She lived in a gloomy old house near the Frauen-Kirche, where she received no society, and led a life as varied and lively on the whole as that of a Trappist. Every Wednesday afternoon we paid a visit to the grave of her "blessed man" in the Protestant cemetery outside the walls, and on Sundays we went three times to church. These were the only breaks in the long monotony of our daily life. On market-days we never went out of doors at all; and when the great annual fair-time came round, we drew down all the front blinds and inhabited the rooms at the back.

As for the pleasures of childhood, I cannot say that I knew many of them in those old Nuremberg days. Still I was not unhappy, nor even very dull. It may be that, knowing nothing pleasanter, I was not even conscious of the dreariness of the atmosphere I breathed. There was, at all events, a big old-fashioned garden full of vegetables and cottage-flowers, at the back of the house, in which I almost lived in Spring and Summer-time, and from which I managed to extract a great deal of enjoyment; while for companions and playmates I had old Karl, my aunt's gardener, a pigeon-house full of pigeons, three staid elderly cats, and a tortoise. In the way of education I fared scantily enough, learning just as little as it pleased my aunt to teach me, and having that little presented to me under its driest and most unattractive aspect.

Such was my life till I went away with my father in the Autumn of 1819. I was then between nine and ten years of age—having lost my mother in earliest infancy, and lived with aunt Martha Baur ever since I could remember.

The change from Nuremberg to Brühl was for me like the transition from Purgatory to Paradise. I enjoyed for the first time all the delights of liberty. I had no lessons to learn; no stern aunt to obey; but, which was infinitely pleasanter, a kind-hearted Rhenish Mädchen, with a silver arrow in her hair, to wait upon me; and an indulgent father whose only orders were that I should be allowed to have my own way in everything.

And my way was to revel in the air and the sunshine; to roam about the park and pleasure-grounds; to watch the soldiers at drill, and hear the band play every day, and wander at will about the deserted state-apartments of the great empty Château.

Looking back upon it from this distance of time, I should pronounce the Electoral Residenz at Brühl to be a miracle of bad taste; but not Aladdin's palace if planted amid the gardens of Armida could then have seemed lovelier in my eyes. The building, a heavy many-windowed pile in the worst style of the worst Renaissance period, stood, and still stands, in a fat, flat country about ten miles from Cologne, to which city it bears much the same relation that Hampton Court bears to London, or Versailles to Paris. Stucco and whitewash had been lavished upon it inside and out, and pallid scagliola did duty everywhere for marble. A grand staircase supported by agonised colossi, grinning and writhing in vain efforts to look as if they didn't mind the weight, led from the great hall to the state apartments; and in these rooms the bad taste of the building may be said to have culminated. Here were mirrors framed in meaningless arabesques, cornices painted to represent bas-reliefs, consoles and pilasters of mock marble, and long generations of Electors in the tawdriest style of portraiture, all at full length, all in their robes of office, and all too evidently by one and the same hand. To me, however, they were all majestic and beautiful. I believed in themselves, their wigs, their armour, their ermine, their high-heeled shoes and their stereotyped smirk, from the earliest to the latest.

But the gardens and grounds were my chief delight, as indeed they were the main attraction of the place, making it the focus of a holiday resort for the townsfolk of Cologne and Bonn, and a point of interest for travellers. First came a great gravelled terrace upon which the ground-floor windows opened—a terrace where the sun shone more fiercely than elsewhere, and orange-trees in tubs bore golden fruit, and great green, yellow, and striped pumpkins, alternating with beds of brilliant white and scarlet geraniums, lay lazily sprawling in the sunshine as if they enjoyed it. Beyond this terrace came vast flats of rich green sward laid out in formal walks, flower-beds and fountains; and beyond these again stretched some two or three miles of finely wooded park, pierced by long avenues that radiated from a common centre and framed in exquisite little far-off views of Falkenlust and the blue hills of the Vorgebirge.

We were lodged at the back, where the private gardens and offices abutted on the village. Our own rooms looked upon our own garden, and upon the church and Franciscan convent beyond. In the warm dusk, when all was still, and my father used to sit smoking his meerschaum by the open window, we could hear the low pealing of the chapel-organ, and the monks chanting their evening litanies.

A happy time — a pleasant, peaceful place! Ah me! how long ago!

2

A whole delightful Summer and Autumn went by thus, and my new home seemed more charming with every change of season. First came the gathering of the golden harvest; then the joyous vintage-time, when the wine-press creaked all day in every open cellar along the village street, and long files of country carts came down from the hills in the dusk evenings, laden with baskets and barrels full of white and purple grapes. And then the long avenues and all the woods of Brühl put on their Autumn robes of crimson, and flame-colour, and golden brown; and the berries reddened in the hedges; and the Autumn burned itself away like a gorgeous sunset; and November came in grey and cold, like the night-time of the year.

I was so happy, however, that I enjoyed even the dull November. I loved the bare avenues carpeted with dead and rustling leaves — the solitary gardens — the long, silent afternoons and evenings when the big logs crackled on the hearth, and my father smoked his pipe in the chimney corner. We had no such wood-fires at Aunt Martha Baur's in those dreary old Nuremberg days, now almost forgotten; but then, to be sure, Aunt Martha Baur, who was a sparing woman and looked after every groschen, had to pay for her own logs, whereas ours were cut from the Crown Woods, and cost not a pfennig.

It was, as well as I can remember, just about this time, when the days were almost at their briefest, that my father received an official communication from Berlin desiring him to make ready a couple of rooms for the immediate reception of a state-prisoner, for whose safe-keeping he would be held responsible till further notice. The letter—(I have it in my desk now)—was folded square, sealed with five seals, and signed in the King's name by the Minister of War; and it was brought, as I well remember, by a mounted orderly from Cologne.

So a couple of empty rooms were chosen on the second story, just over one of the State apartments at the end of the east wing; and my father, who was by no means well pleased with his office, set to work to ransack the Château for furniture.

"Since it is the King's pleasure to make a gaoler of me," said he, "I'll try to give my poor devil of a prisoner all the comforts I can. Come with me, my little Gretchen, and let's see what chairs and tables we can find up in the garrets."

Now I had been longing to explore the top rooms ever since I came to live at Brühl—those top rooms under the roof, of which the shutters were always closed, and the doors always locked, and where not even the housemaids were admitted oftener than twice a year. So at this welcome invitation I sprang up, joyfully enough, and ran before my father all the way. But when he unlocked the first door, and all beyond was dark, and the air that met us on the threshold had a faint and dead odour, like the atmosphere of a tomb, I shrank back trembling, and dared not venture in. Nor did my courage altogether come back when the shutters were thrown open, and the wintry sunlight streamed in upon dusty floors, and cobwebbed ceilings, and piles of mysterious objects covered in a ghostly way with large white sheets, looking like heaps of slain upon a funeral pyre.

The slain, however, turned out to be the very things of which we were in search; old-fashioned furniture in all kinds of incongruous styles, and of all epochs—Louis Quatorze cabinets in cracked tortoise-shell and blackened buhl—antique carved chairs emblazoned elaborately with coats of arms, as old as the time of Albert Dürer— slender-legged tables in battered marqueterie—time-pieces in lacklustre ormolu, still pointing to the hour at which they had stopped, who could tell how many years ago? bundles of moth-eaten tapestries and faded silken hangings—exquisite oval mirrors framed in chipped wreaths of delicate Dresden china—mouldering old portraits of dead-and-gone court beauties in powder and patches, warriors in wigs, and prelates in point-lace—whole suites of furniture in old stamped leather and worm-eaten Utrecht velvet; broken toilette services in pink and blue Sèvres; screens, wardrobes, cornices—in short, all kinds of luxurious lumber going fast to dust, like those who once upon a time enjoyed and owned it.

And now, going from room to room, we chose a chair here, a table there, and so on, till we had enough to furnish a bedroom and sitting-room.

"He must have a writing-table," said my father, thoughtfully, "and a book-case."

Saying which, he stopped in front of a ricketty-looking gilded cabinet with empty red-velvet shelves, and tapped it with his cane.

"But supposing he has no books!" suggested I, with the precocious wisdom of nine years of age.

"Then we must beg some, or borrow some, my little Mädchen," replied my father, gravely; "for books are the main solace of the captive, and he who hath them not lies in a twofold prison."

"He shall have my picture-book of Hartz legends!" said I, in a sudden impulse of compassion. Whereupon my father took me up in his arms, kissed me on both cheeks, and bade me choose some knicknacks for the prisoner's sitting-room.

"For though we have gotten together all the necessaries for comfort, we have taken nothing for adornment," said he, "and 'twere pity the prison were duller than it need be. Choose thou a pretty face or two from among these old pictures, my little Gretchen, and an ornament for his mantelshelf. Young as thou art, thou hast the woman's wit in thee."

So I picked out a couple of Sèvres candlesticks; a painted Chinese screen, all pagodas and parrots; two portraits of patched and powdered beauties in the Watteau style; and a queer old clock surmounted by a gilt Cupid in a chariot drawn by doves. If these failed to make him happy, thought I, he must indeed be hard to please.

That afternoon, the things having been well dusted, and the rooms thoroughly cleaned, we set to work to arrange the furniture, and so quickly was this done that before we sat down to supper the place was ready for occupation, even to the logs upon the hearth and the oil-lamp upon the table.

All night my dreams were of the prisoner. I was seeking him in the gloom of the upper rooms, or amid the dusky mazes of the leaf-less plantations — always seeing him afar off, never overtaking him, and trying in vain to catch a glimpse of his features. But his face was always turned from me.

My first words on waking, were to ask if he had yet come. All day long I was waiting, and watching, and listening for him, starting up at every sound, and continually running to the window. Would he be young and handsome? Or would he be old, and white-haired, and world-forgotten, like some of those Bastille prisoners I had heard my father speak of? Would his chains rattle when he walked about? I asked myself these questions, and answered them as my childish imagination prompted, a hundred times a day; and still he came not.

So another twenty-four hours went by, and my impatience was almost beginning to wear itself out, when at last, about five o'clock in the afternoon of the third day, it being already quite dark, there came a sudden clanging of the gates, followed by a rattle of wheels in the courtyard, and a hurrying to and fro of feet upon the stairs.

Then, listening with a beating heart, but seeing nothing, I knew that he was come.

I had to sleep that night with my curiosity ungratified; for my father had hurried away at the first sounds from without, nor came back till long after I had been carried off to bed by my Rhenish handmaiden.

3

He was neither old nor white-haired. He was, as well as I, in my childish way could judge, about thirty-five years of age, pale, slight, dark-eyed, delicate-looking. His chains did not rattle as he walked, for the simple reason that, being a prisoner on parole, he suffered no kind of restraint, but was as free as myself of the Château and grounds. He wore his hair long, tied behind with a narrow black ribbon, and very slightly powdered; and he dressed always in deep mourning—black, all black, from head to foot, even to his shoe-buckles. He was a Frenchman, and he went by the name of Monsieur Maurice.

I cannot tell how I knew that this was only his Christian name; but so it was, and I knew him by no other, neither did my father. I have, indeed, evidence among our private papers to show that neither by those in authority at Berlin, nor by the prisoner himself, was he at any time informed either of the family name of Monsieur Maurice, or of the nature of the offence, whether military or political, for which that gentleman was consigned to his keeping at Brühl.

"Of one thing at least I am certain," said my father, holding out his pipe for me to fill it. "He is a soldier."

It was just after dinner, the second day following our prisoner's arrival, and I was sitting on my father's knee before the fire, as was our pleasant custom of an afternoon.

"I see it in his eye," my father went on to say. "I see it in his walk. I see it in the way he arranges his papers on the table. Everything in order. Everything put away into the smallest possible compass. All this bespeaketh the camp."

"I don't believe he is a soldier, for all that," said I, thoughtfully. "He is too gentle."

"The bravest soldiers, my little Gretchen, are ofttimes the gentlest," replied my father. "The great French hero, Bayard, and the great English hero, Sir Philip Sidney, about whom thou wert reading 'tother day, were both as tender and gentle as women."

"But he neither smokes, nor swears, nor talks loud," said I, persisting in my opinion.

My father smiled, and pinched my ear.

"Nay, little one," said he, "Monsieur Maurice is not like thy father—a rough German Dragoon risen from the ranks. He is a gentleman, and a Frenchman; and he hath all the polish of what the Frenchman calls the *vieille école*. And there again he puzzles me with his court-manners and his powdered hair! He's no Bonapartist, I'll be sworn—yet if he be o' the King's side, what doth he here, with the usurper at Saint Helena, and Louis the Eighteenth come to his own again?"

"But he *is* a Bonapartist, father," said I, "for he carries the Emperor's portrait on his snuff-box."

My father laid down his pipe, and drew a long breath expressive of astonishment.

"He showed thee his snuff-box!" exclaimed he.

"Ay—and told me it was the Emperor's own gift."

"Thunder and Mars! And when was this, my little Gretchen?"

"Yesterday morning, on the terrace. And he asked my name; and told me I should go up some day to his room and see his sketches; and he kissed me when he said good-bye; and—and I like Monsieur Maurice very much, father, and I'm sure it's very wicked of the King to keep him here in prison!"

My father looked at me, shook his head, and twirled his long grey moustache.

"Bonapartist or Legitimist, again I say what doth he here?" muttered he presently, more to himself than to me. "If Legitimist, why not with his King? If Bonapartist—then he is his King's prisoner; not ours. It passeth my comprehension how we should hold him at Brühl."

"Let him run away, father dear, and don't run after him!" whispered I, putting my arms coaxingly about his neck.

"But 'tis some cursed mess of politics at bottom, depend on't!" continued my father, still talking to himself. "Ah, you don't know what politics are, my little Gretchen! — so much the better for you!"

"I do know what politics are," replied I, with great dignity. "They are the *chef-d'oeuvre* of Satan. I heard you say so the other day."

My father burst into a Titanic roar of laughter.

"Said I so?" shouted he. "Thunder and Mars! I did not remember that I had ever said anything half so epigrammatic!"

Now from this it will be seen that the prisoner and I were already acquainted. We had, indeed, taken to each other from the first, and our mutual liking ripened so rapidly that before a week was gone by we had become the fastest friends in the world.

Our first meeting, as I have already said, took place upon the terrace. Our second, which befell on the afternoon of the same day when my father and I had held the conversation just recorded, happened on the stairs. Monsieur Maurice was coming up with his hat on; I was running down. He stopped, and held out both his hands.

"*Bonjour, petite,*" he said, smiling. "Whither away so fast?"

The hoar frost was clinging to his coat, where he had brushed against the trees in his walk, and he looked pale and tired.

"I am going home," I replied.

"Home? Did you not tell me you lived in the Château?"

"So I do, Monsieur; but at the other side, up the other staircase. This is the side of the state-apartments."

Then, seeing in his face a look half of surprise, half of curiosity, I added: —

"I often go there in the afternoon, when it is too cold, or too late for out-of-doors. They are such beautiful rooms, and full of such beautiful pictures! Would you like to see them?"

He smiled, and shook his head.

"Thanks, petite," he said, "I am too cold now, and too tired; but you shall show them to me some other day. Meanwhile, suppose you come up and pay me that promised visit?"

I assented joyfully, and slipping my hand into his with the ready confidence of childhood, turned back at once and went with him to his rooms on the second floor.

Here, finding the fire in the salon nearly out, we went down upon our knees and blew the embers with our breath, and laughed so merrily over our work that by the time the new logs had caught, I was as much at home as if I had known Monsieur Maurice all my life.

"*Tiens!*" he said, taking me presently upon his knee and brushing the specks of white ash from my clothes and hair, "what a little Cinderella I have made of my guest! This must not happen again, Gretchen. Did you not tell me yesterday that your name was Gretchen?"

"Yes, but Gretchen, you know, is not my real name," said I, "my real name is Marguerite. Gretchen is only my pet name."

"Then you will always be Gretchen for me," said Monsieur Maurice, with the sweetest smile in the world.

There were books upon the table; there was a thing like a telescope on a brass stand in the window; there was a guitar lying on the couch. The fire, too, was burning brightly now, and the room altogether wore a cheerful air of habitation.

"It looks more like a lady's boudoir than a prison," said Monsieur Maurice, reading my thoughts. "I wonder whose rooms they were before I came here!"

"They were nobody's rooms," said I. "They were quite empty."

And then I told him where we had found the furniture, and how the ornamental part thereof had been of my choosing.

"I don't know who the ladies are," I said, referring to the portraits. "I only chose them for their pretty faces."

"Their lovers probably did the same, petite, a hundred years ago," replied
Monsieur Maurice. "And the clock—did you choose that also?"

"Yes; but the clock doesn't go."

"So much the better. I would that time might stand still also—till I am free! till I am free!"

The tears rushed to my eyes. It was the tone more than the words that touched my heart. He stooped and kissed me on the forehead.

"Come to the window, little one," said he, "and I will show you something very beautiful. Do you know what this is?"

"A telescope!"

"No; a solar microscope. Now look down into this tube, and tell me what you see. A piece of Persian carpet? No—a butterfly's wing magnified hundreds and hundreds of times. And this which looks like an aigrette of jewels? Will you believe that it is just the tiny plume which waves on the head of every little gnat that buzzes round you on a Summer's evening?"

I uttered exclamation after exclamation of delight. Every fresh object seemed more wonderful and beautiful than the last, and I felt as if I could go on looking down that magic tube for ever. Meanwhile Monsieur Maurice, whose good-nature was at least as inexhaustible as my curiosity, went on changing the slides till we had gone through a whole boxfull.

By this time it was getting rapidly dusk, and I could see no longer.

"You will show me some more another day?" said I, giving up reluctantly.

"That I will, petite, I have at least a dozen more boxes full of slides."

"And—and you said I should see your sketches, Monsieur Maurice."

"All in good time, little Gretchen," he said, smiling. "All in good time. See—those are the sketches, in yonder folio; that mahogany case under the couch contains a collection of gems in glass and paste; those red books in the bookcase are full of pictures. You shall see them all by degrees; but only by degrees. For if I did not keep something back to tempt my little guest, she would not care to visit the solitary prisoner."

I felt myself colour crimson.

"But—but indeed I would care to come, Monsieur Maurice, if you had nothing at all to show me," I said, half hurt, half angry.

He gave me a strange look that I could not understand, and stroked my hair caressingly.

"Come often, then, little one," he said. "Come very often; and when we are tired of pictures and microscopes, we will sit upon the floor, and tell sad stories of the deaths of kings."

Then, seeing my look puzzled, he laughed and added:—

"'Tis a great English poet says that, Gretchen, in one of his plays."

Here a shrill trumpet-call in the court-yard, followed by the pro-longed roll of many drums, warned me that evening parade was called, and that as soon as it was over my father would be home and looking for me. So I started up, and put out my hand to say good-bye.

Monsieur Maurice took it between both his own.

"I don't like parting from you so soon, little Mädchen," he said. "Will you come again to-morrow?"

"Every day, if you like!" I replied eagerly.

"Then every day it shall be; and—let me see—you shall improve my bad
German, and I will teach you French."

I could have clapped my hands for joy. I was longing to learn French, and I knew how much it would also please my father; so I thanked Monsieur Maurice again and again, and ran home with a light heart to tell of all the wonders I had seen.

4

From this time forth, I saw him always once, and sometimes twice a day—in the afternoons, when he regularly gave me the promised French lesson; and occasionally in the mornings, provided the weather was neither too cold nor too damp for him to join me in the grounds. For Monsieur Maurice was not strong. He could not with impunity face snow, and rain, and our keen Rhenish north-east winds; and it was only when the wintry sun shone out at noon and the air came tempered from the south, that he dared venture from his own fire-side. When, however, there shone a sunny day, with what delight I used to summon him for a walk, take him to my favourite points of view, and show him the woodland nooks that had been my chosen haunts in summer! Then, too, the unwonted colour would come back to his pale cheek, and the smile to his lips, and while the ramble and the sunshine lasted he would be all jest and gaiety, pelting me with dead leaves, chasing me in and out of the plantations, and telling me strange stories, half pathetic, half grotesque, of Dryads, and Fauns, and Satyrs—of Bacchus, and Pan, and Polyphemus—of nymphs who became trees, and shepherds who were transformed to fountains, and all kinds of beautiful wild myths of antique Greece—far more beautiful and far more wild than all the tales of gnomes and witches in my book of Hartz legends.

At other times, when the weather was cold or rainy, he would take down his "Musée Napoléon," a noble work in eight or ten volumes, and show me engravings after pictures by great masters in the Louvre, explaining them to me as we went along, painting in words the glow and glory of the absent colour, and steeping my childish imagination in golden dreams of Raphael and Titian, and Paulo Veronese.

And sometimes, too, as the dusk came on and the firelight brightened in the gathering gloom, he would take up his guitar, and to the accompaniment of a few slight chords sing me a quaint old French chanson of the feudal times; or an Arab chant picked up in the tent or the Nile boat; or a Spanish ballad, half love-song, half litany, learned from the lips of a muleteer on the Pyrenean border.

For Monsieur Maurice, whatever his present adversities, had travelled far and wide at some foregone period of his life—in Syria, and Persia; in northernmost Tartary and the Siberian steppes; in Egypt and the Nubian desert, and among the perilous wilds of central Arabia. He spoke and wrote with facility some ten or twelve languages. He drew admirably, and had a profound knowledge of the Italian schools of art; and his memory was a rich storehouse of adventure and anecdote, legend and song.

I am an old woman now, and Monsieur Maurice must have passed away many a year ago upon his last long journey; but even at this distance of time, my eyes are dimmed with tears when I remember how he used to unlock that storehouse for my pleasure, and ransack his memory for stories either of his own personal perils by flood and field, or of the hairbreadth 'scapes of earlier travellers. For it was his amusement to amuse me; his happiness to make me happy. And I in return loved him with all my childish heart. Nay, with something deeper and more romantic than a childish love — say rather with that kind of passionate hero-worship which is an attribute more of youth than of childhood, and, like the quality of mercy, blesseth him that gives even more than him that takes.

"What dreadful places you have travelled in, Monsieur Maurice!" I exclaimed one day. "What dangers you have seen!"

He had been showing me a little sketchbook full of Eastern jottings, and had just explained how a certain boat therein depicted had upset with him on a part of the Upper Nile so swarming with alligators that he had to swim for his life, and even so, barely scrambled up the slimy bank in time.

"He who travels far courts many kinds of death," replied Monsieur Maurice; "but he escapes that which is worst—death from ennui."

"Suppose they had dragged you back, when you were half way up the bank!" said I, shuddering.

And as I spoke, I felt myself turn pale; for I could see the brown monsters crowding to shore, and the red glitter of their cruel eyes and the hot breath steaming from their open jaws.

"Then they would have eaten me up as easily as you might swallow an oyster," laughed Monsieur Maurice. "Nay, my child, why that serious face? I should have escaped a world of trouble, and been missed by no one—except poor Ali."

"Who was Ali?" I asked quickly.

"Ali was my Nubian servant—my only friend, then; as you, little Gretchen, are my only friend, now," replied Monsieur Maurice, sadly. "Aye, my only little friend in the wide world—and I think a true one."

I did not know what to say; but I nestled closer to his side; and pressed my cheek up fondly against his shoulder.

"Tell me more about him, Monsieur Maurice," I whispered. "I am so glad he loved you dearly."

"He loved me very dearly," said Monsieur Maurice "so dearly that he gave his life for me."

"But is Ali dead?"

"Ay—Ali is dead. Nay, his story is brief enough, petite. I bought him in the slave market at Cairo—a poor, sickly, soulless lad, half stupid from ill-treatment. I gave him good food, good clothes, and liberty. I taught him to read. I made him my own servant; and his soul and his strength came back to him as if by a miracle. He became stalwart and intelligent, and so faithful that he was ten times more my slave than if I had held him to his bondage. I took him with me through all my Eastern pilgrimage. He was my body-guard; my cook; my dragoman; everything. He slept on a mat at the foot of my bed every night, like a dog. So he lived with me for nearly four years—till I lost him."

He paused.

I did not dare to ask, "what more?" but waited breathlessly.

"The rest is soon told," he said presently; but in an altered voice. "It happened in Ceylon. Our way lay along a bridle-path overhanging a steep gorge on the one hand and skirting the jungle on the other. Do you know what the jungle is, little Gretchen? Fancy an untrodden wilderness where huge trees, matted together by trailing creepers of gigantic size, shut out the sun and make a green roof of inextricable shade—where the very grass grows taller than the tallest man—where apes chatter, and parrots scream, and deadly reptiles swarm; and where nature has run wild since ever the world began. Well, so we went—I on my horse; Ali at my bridle; two porters following with food and baggage; the precipice below; the forest above; the morning sun just risen over all. On a sudden, Ali held his breath and listened. His practised ear had caught a sound that mine could not detect. He seized my rein—forced my horse back upon his haunches—drew his hunting knife, and ran forward to reconnoitre. The turn of the road hid him for a moment from my sight. The next instant, I had sprung from the saddle, pistol in hand, and run after him to share the sport or the danger. My little Gretchen—he was gone."

"Gone!" I echoed.

Monsieur Maurice shook his head, and turned his face away.

"I heard a crashing and crackling of the underwood," he said; "a faint moan dying on the sultry air. I saw a space of dusty road trampled over with prints of an enormous paw—a tiny trail of blood—a shred of silken fringe—and nothing more. He was gone."

"What was it?" I asked presently, in an awestruck whisper.

Monsieur Maurice, instead of answering my question, opened the sketch-book at a page full of little outlines of animals and birds, and laid his finger silently on the figure of a sleeping tiger.

I shuddered.

"*Pauvre petite!*" he said, shutting up the book, "it is too terrible a story. I ought not to have told it to you. Try to forget it."

"Ah, no!" I said. "I shall never forget it, Monsieur Maurice. Poor Ali! Have you still the piece of fringe you found lying in the road?"

He unlocked his desk and touched a secret spring; whereupon a small drawer flew out from a recess just under the lock.

"Here it is," he said, taking out a piece of folded paper.

It contained the thing he had described—a scrap of fringe composed of crimson and yellow twist, about two inches in length.

"And those other things?" I said, peering into the secret drawer with a child's inquisitiveness. "Have they a history, too?"

Monsieur Maurice hesitated—took them out—sighed—and said, somewhat reluctantly:—

"You may see them, little Gretchen, if you will. Yes; they, too, have their history—but let it be. We have had enough sad stories for to-day."

Those other things, as I had called them, were a withered rose in a little cardboard box, and a miniature of a lady in a purple morocco case.

5

It so happened that the Winter this year was unusually severe, not only at Brühl and the parts about Cologne, but throughout all the Rhine country. Heavy snows fell at Christmas and lay unmelted for weeks upon the ground. Long forgotten sleighs were dragged out from their hiding places and put upon the road, not only for the transport of goods, but for the conveyance of passengers. The ponds in every direction and all the smaller streams were fast frozen. Great masses of dirty ice, too, came floating down the Rhine, and there were rumours of the great river being quite frozen over somewhere up in Switzerland, many hundred miles nearer its source.

For myself, I enjoyed it all—the bitter cold, the short days, the rapid exercise, the blazing fires within, and the glittering snow without. I made snow-men and snow-castles to my heart's content. I learned to skate with my father on the frozen ponds. I was never weary of admiring the wintry landscape—the wide plains sheeted with silver; the purple mountains peeping through brown vistas of bare forest; the nearer trees standing out in featherlike tracery against the blue-green sky. To me it was all beautiful; even more beautiful than in the radiant summertime.

Not so, however, was it with Monsieur Maurice. Racked by a severe cough and unable to leave the house for weeks together, he suffered intensely all the winter through. He suffered in body, and he suffered also in mind. I could see that he was very sad, and that there were times when the burden of life was almost more than he knew how to bear. He had brought with him, as I have shown, certain things wherewith to alleviate the weariness of captivity—books, music, drawing materials, and the like; but I soon discovered that the books were his only solace, and that he never took up pencil or guitar, unless for my amusement.

He wrote a great deal, however, and so consumed many a weary hour of the twenty-four. He used a thick yellowish paper cut quite square, and wrote a very small, neat, upright hand, as clear and legible as print. Every time I found him at his desk and saw those closely covered pages multiplying under his hand, I used to wonder what he could have to write about, and for whose eyes that elaborate manuscript was intended.

"How cold you are, Monsieur Maurice!" I used to say. "You are as cold as my snow-man in the court-yard! Won't you come out to-day for half-an-hour?"

And his hands, in truth, were always ice-like, even though the hearth was heaped with blazing logs.

"Not to-day, petite," he would reply. "It is too bleak for me—and besides, you see, I am writing."

It was his invariable reply. He was always writing—or if not writing, reading; or brooding listlessly over the fire. And so he grew paler every day.

"But the writing can wait, Monsieur Maurice," I urged one morning, "and you can't always be reading the same old books over and over again!"

"Some books never grow old, little Gretchen," he replied. "This, for instance, is quite new; and yet it was written by one Horatius Flaccus somewhere about eighteen hundred years ago."

"But the sun is really shining this morning, Monsieur Maurice!"

"*Comment!*" he said, smiling. "Do you think to persuade me that yonder is the sun—the great, golden, glorious, bountiful sun? No, no, my child! Where I come from, we have the only true sun, and believe in no other!"

"But you come from France, don't you, Monsieur Maurice?" I asked quickly.

"From the South of France, petite—from the France of palms, and orange-groves, and olives; where the myrtle flowers at Christmas, and the roses bloom all the year round!"

"But that must be where Paradise was, Monsieur Maurice!" I exclaimed.

"Ay; it was Paradise once—for me," he said, with a sigh.

Thus, after a moment's pause, he went on:—

"The house in which I was born stands on a low cliff above the sea. It is an old, old house, with all kinds of quaint little turrets, and gable ends, and picturesque nooks and corners about it—such as one sees in most French Châteaux of that period; and it lies back somewhat, with a great rambling garden stretching out between it and the edge of the cliff. Three *berceaux* of orange-trees lead straight away from the paved terrace on which the salon windows open, to another terrace overhanging the beach and the sea. The cliff is overgrown from top to bottom with shrubs and wild flowers, and a flight of steps cut in the living rock leads down to a little cove and a strip of yellow sand a hundred feet below. Ah, petite, I fancy I can see myself scrambling up and down those steps—a child younger than yourself; watching the sun go down into that purple sea; counting the sails in the offing at early morn; and building castles with that yellow sand, just as you build castles out yonder with the snow!"

I clasped my hands and listened breathlessly.

"Oh, Monsieur Maurice," I said, "I did not think there was such a beautiful place in the world! It sounds like a fairy tale."

He smiled, sighed, and—being seated at his desk with the pen in his hand—took up a blank sheet of paper, and began sketching the Château and the cliff.

"Tell me more about it, Monsieur Maurice," I pleaded coaxingly.

"What more can I tell you, little one? See—this window in the turret to the left was my bed-room window, and here, just below, was my study, where as a boy I prepared my lessons for my tutor. That large Gothic window under the gable was the window of the library."

"And is it all just like that still?" I asked.

"I don't know," he said dreamily. "I suppose so."

He was now putting in the rocks, and the rough steps leading down to the beach.

"Had you any little brothers and sisters, Monsieur Maurice?" I asked next; for my interest and curiosity were unbounded.

He shook his head.

"None," he said, "none whatever. I was an only child; and I am the last of my name."

I longed to question him further, but did not dare to do so.

"You will go back there some day, Monsieur Maurice," I said hesitatingly, "when—when—"

"When I am free, little Gretchen? Ah! who can tell? Besides the old place is no longer mine. They have taken it from me, and given it to a stranger."

"Taken it from you, Monsieur Maurice!" I exclaimed indignantly.

"Ay; but—who knows? We see strange changes. Where a king reigns to-day, an emperor, or a mob, may rule to-morrow."

He spoke more to himself than to me, but I had some dim understanding, nevertheless, of what he meant.

He had by this time drawn the cliff, and the strip of sand, and the waste of sea beyond; and now he was blotting in some boats and figures—figures of men wading through the surf and dragging the boats in shore; and other figures making for the steps. Last of all, close under the cliff, in advance of all the rest, he drew a tiny man standing alone—a tiny man scarce an eighth of an inch in height, struck out with three or four touches of the pen, and yet so full of character that one knew at a glance he was the leader of the others. I saw the outstretched arm in act of command—I recognised the well-known cocked hat—the general outline of a figure already familiar to me in a hundred prints, and I exclaimed, almost involuntarily:—

"Bonaparte!"

Monsieur Maurice started; shot a quick, half apprehensive glance at me; crumpled the drawing up in his hand, and flung it into the fire.

"Oh, Monsieur Maurice!" I cried, "what have you done?"

"It was a mere scrawl," he said impatiently.

"No, no—it was beautiful. I would have given anything for it!"

Monsieur Maurice laughed, and patted me on the cheek.

"Nonsense, petite, nonsense!" he said. "It was only fit for the fire. I will make you a better drawing, if you remind me of it, to-morrow."

When I told this to my father—and I used to prattle to him a good deal about Monsieur Maurice at supper, in those days—he tugged at his moustache, and shook his head, and looked very grave indeed.

"The South of France!" he muttered, "the South of France! *Sacré coeur d'une bombe*! Why, the usurper, when he came from Elba, landed on that coast somewhere near Cannes!"

"And went to Monsieur Maurice's house, father!" I cried, "and that is why the King of France has taken Monsieur Maurice's house away from him, and given it to a stranger! I am sure that's it! I see it all now!"

But my father only shook his head again, and looked still more grave.

"No, no, no," he said, "neither all—nor half—nor a quarter! There's more behind. I don't understand it—I don't understand it. Thunder and Mars! Why don't we hand him over to the French Government? That's what puzzles me."

6

The severity of the Winter had, I think, in some degree abated, and the snowdrops were already above ground, when again a mounted orderly rode in from Cologne, bringing another official letter for the Governor of Brühl.

Now my father's duties as Governor of Brühl were very light—so light that he had not found it necessary to set apart any special room, or bureau, for the transaction of such business as might be connected therewith. When, therefore, letters had to be written or accounts made up, he wrote those letters and made up those accounts at a certain large writing-table, fitted with drawers, pigeon-holes, and a shelf for account-books, that stood in a corner of our sitting-room. Here also, if any persons had to be received, he received them. To this day, whenever I go back in imagination to those bygone times, I seem to see my father sitting at that writing-table nibbling the end of his pen, and one of the sergeants off guard perched on the edge of a chair close against the door, with his hat on his knees, waiting for orders.

There being, as I have said, no especial room set apart for business purposes, the orderly was shown straight to our own room, and there delivered his despatch. It was about a quarter past one. We had dined, and my father had just brought out his pipe. The door leading into our little dining-room was, indeed, standing wide open, and the dishes were still upon the table.

My father took the despatch, turned it over, broke the seals one by one (there were five of them, as before), and read it slowly through. As he read, a dark cloud seemed to settle on his brow.

Then he looked up frowning—seemed about to speak—checked himself—and read the despatch over again.

"From whose hands did you receive this?" he said abruptly.

"From General Berndorf, Excellency," stammered the orderly, carrying his hand to his cap.

"Is his Excellency the Baron von Bulow at Cologne?"

"I have not heard so, Excellency."

"Then this despatch came direct from Berlin, and has been forwarded from

Cologne?"

"Yes, Excellency."

"How did it come from Berlin? By mail, or by special messenger?"

"By special messenger, Excellency."

Now General Berndorf was the officer in command of the garrison at Cologne, and the Baron von Bulow, as I well knew, was His Majesty's Minister of War at Berlin.

Having received these answers, my father stood silent, as if revolving some difficult matter in his thoughts. Then, his mind being made up, he turned again to the orderly and said: —

"Dine—feed your horse—and come back in an hour for the answer."

Thankful to be dismissed, the man saluted and vanished. My father had a rapid, stern way of speaking to subordinates, that had in general the effect of making them glad to get out of his presence as quickly as possible.

Then he read the despatch for the third time; turned to his writing-table; dropped into his chair; and prepared to write.

But the task, apparently, was not easy. Watching him from the fireside corner where I was sitting on a low stool with an open story-book upon my lap, I saw him begin and tear up three separate attempts. The fourth, however, seemed to be more successful. Once written, he read it over, copied it carefully, called to me for a light, sealed his letter, and addressed it to "His Excellency the Baron von Bulow."

This done, he enclosed it under cover to "General Berndorf, Cologne"; and had just sealed the outer cover when the orderly came back. My father gave it to him with scarcely a word, and two minutes after, we heard him clattering out of the courtyard at a hand-gallop.

Then my father came back to his chair by the fireside, lit his pipe, and sat thinking silently. I looked up in his face, but felt, somehow, that I must not speak to him; for the cloud was still there, and his thoughts were far away. Presently his pipe went out; but he held it still, unconscious and absorbed. In all the months we had been living at Brühl I had never seen him look so troubled.

So he sat, and so he looked for a long time—for perhaps the greater part
of an hour—during which I could think of nothing but the despatch, and
Monsieur Maurice, and the Minister of War; for that it all had to do with
Monsieur Maurice I never doubted for an instant.

By just such another despatch, sealed and sent in precisely the same way, and from the same person, his coming hither had been heralded. How, then, should not this one concern him? And in what way would he be affected by it? Seeing that dark look in my father's face, I knew not what to think or what to fear.

At length, after what had seemed to me an interval of interminable silence, the time-piece in the corner struck half-past three—the hour at which Monsieur Maurice was accustomed to give me the daily French lesson; so I got up quietly and stole towards the door, knowing that I was expected upstairs.

"Where are you going, Gretchen?" said my father, sharply.

It was the first time he had opened his lips since the orderly had clattered out of the courtyard.

"I am going up to Monsieur Maurice," I replied.

My father shook his head.

"Not to-day, my child," he said, "not to-day. I have business with Monsieur
Maurice this afternoon. Stay here till I come back."

And with this he got up, took his hat and went quickly out of the room.

So I waited and waited—as it seemed to me for hours. The waning day-light faded and became dusk; the dusk thickened into dark;

the fire burned red and dull; and still I crouched there in the chimney-corner. I had no heart to read, work, or fan the logs into a blaze. I just watched the clock, and waited. When the room became so dark that I could see the hands no longer, I counted the strokes of the pendulum, and told the quarters off upon my fingers.

When at length my father came back, it was past five o'clock, and dark as midnight.

"Quick, quick, little Gretchen," he said, pulling off his hat and gloves, and unbuckling his sword. "A glass of kirsch, and more logs on the fire! I am cold through and through, and wet into the bargain."

"But—but, father, have you not been with Monsieur Maurice?" I said, anxiously.

"Yes, of course; but that was an hour ago, and more. I have been over to
Kierberg since then, in the rain."

He had left Monsieur Maurice an hour ago—a whole, wretched, dismal hour, during which I might have been so happy!

"You told me to stay here till you came back," I said, scarce able to keep down the tears that started to my eyes.

"Well, my little Mädchen?"

"And—and I might have gone up to Monsieur Maurice, after all?"

My father looked at me gravely—poured out a second glass of kirsch—drew his chair to the front of the fire, and said:—

"I don't know about that, Gretchen."

I had felt all along that there was something wrong, and now I was certain of it.

"What do you mean, father?" I said, my heart beating so that I could scarcely speak. "What is the matter?"

"May the devil make broth of my bones, if I know!" said my father, tugging savagely at his moustache.

"But there is something!"

He nodded, grimly.

"Monsieur Maurice, it seems, is not to have so much liberty," he said, after a moment. "He is not to walk in the grounds oftener than twice a week; and then only with a soldier at his heels. And he is not to go beyond half a mile from the Château in any direction. And he is to hold no communication whatever with any person, or persons, either in-doors or out-of-doors, except such as are in direct charge of his rooms or his person. And—and heaven knows what other confounded regulations besides! I wish the Baron von Bulow had been in Spitzbergen before he put it into the King's head to send him here at all!"

"But—but he is not to be locked up?" I faltered, almost in a whisper.

"Well, no—not exactly that; but I am to post a sentry in the corridor, outside his door."

"Then the King is afraid that Monsieur Maurice will run away!"

"I don't know—I suppose so," groaned my father.

I sat silent for a moment, and then burst into a flood of tears.

"Poor Monsieur Maurice!" I cried. "He has coughed so all the Winter; and he was longing for the Spring! We were to have gathered primroses in the woods when the warm days came back again—and—and—and I suppose the King doesn't mean that I am not to speak to him any more!"

My sobs choked me, and I could say no more.

My father took me on his knee, and tried to comfort me.

"Don't cry, my little Gretchen," he said tenderly; "don't cry! Tears can help neither the prisoner nor thee."

"But I may go to him all the same, father?" I pleaded.

"By my sword, I don't know," stammered my father. "If it were a breach of orders … and yet for a baby like thee … thou'rt no more than a mouse about the room, after all!"

"I have read of a poor prisoner who broke his heart because the gaoler killed a spider he loved," said I, through my tears.

My father's features relaxed into a smile.

"But do you flatter yourself that Monsieur Maurice loves my little Mädchen as much as that poor prisoner loved his spider?" he said, taking me by the ear.

"Of course he does—and a hundred thousand times better!" I exclaimed, not without a touch of indignation.

My father laughed outright.

"Thunder and Mars!" said he, "is the case so serious? Then Monsieur Maurice, I suppose, must be allowed sometimes to see his little pet spider."

He took me up himself next morning to the prisoner's room, and then for the first time I found a sentry in occupation of the corridor. He grounded his musket and saluted as we passed.

"I bring you a visitor, Monsieur Maurice," said my father.

He was leaning over the fire in a moody attitude when we went in, with his arms on the chimney-piece, but turned at the first sound of my father's voice.

"Colonel Bernhard," he said, with a look of glad surprise, "this is kind,
I—I had scarcely dared to hope"....

He said no more, but took me by both hands, and kissed me on the forehead.

"I trust I'm not doing wrong," said my father gruffly. "I hope it's not a breach of orders."

"I am sure it is not," replied Monsieur Maurice, still holding my hands. "Were your instructions twice as strict, they could not be supposed to apply to this little maiden."

"They are strict enough, Monsieur Maurice," said my father, drily.

A faint flush rose to the prisoner's cheek.

"I know it," he said. "And they are as unnecessary as they are strict. I had given you my parole, Colonel Bernhard."

My father pulled at his moustache, and looked uncomfortable.

"I'm sure you would have kept it, Monsieur Maurice," he said.

Monsieur Maurice bowed.

"I wish it, however, to be distinctly understood," he said, "that I withdrew that parole from the moment when a sentry was stationed at my door."

"Naturally—naturally."

"And, for my papers"....

"I wish to heaven they had said nothing about them!" interrupted my father, impatiently.

"Thanks. 'Tis a petty tyranny; but it cannot be helped. Since, however, you are instructed to seize them, here they are. They contain neither political nor private matter—as you will see."

"I shall see nothing of the kind, Monsieur Maurice," said my father. "I would not read a line of them for a marshal's bâton. The King must make a gaoler of me, if it so pleases him; but not a spy. I shall seal up the papers and send them to Berlin."

"And I shall never see my manuscript again!" said Monsieur Maurice, with a sigh. "Well—it was my first attempt at authorship— perhaps, my last—and there is an end to it!"

My father ground some new and tremendous oath between his teeth.

"I hate to take it, Monsieur Maurice," he said. "'Tis an odious office."

"The office alone is yours, Colonel Bernhard," said the prisoner, with all a Frenchman's grace. "The odium rests with those who impose it on you."

Hereupon they exchanged formal salutations; and my father, having warned me not to be late for our mid-day meal, put the papers in his pocket, and left me to take my daily French lesson.

7

The Winter lingered long, but the Spring came at last in a burst of sunshine. The grey mists were rent away, as if by magic. The cold hues vanished from the landscape. The earth became all freshness; the air all warmth; the sky all light. The hedgerows caught a tint of tender green. The crocuses came up in a single night. The woods which till now had remained bare and brown, flushed suddenly, as if the coming Summer were imprisoned in their glowing buds. The birds began to try their little voices here and there. Never once, in all the years that have gone by since then, have I seen so startling a transition. It was as if the Prince in the dear old fairy tale had just kissed the Sleeping Beauty, and all that enchanted world had sprung into life at the meeting of their lips.

But the Spring, with its sudden beauty and brightness, seems to have no charm for Monsieur Maurice. He has permission to walk in the grounds twice a week—with a sentry at his heels; but of that permission he sternly refuses to take advantage. It was not wonderful that he preferred his fireside and his books, while the sleet, and snow, and bitter east winds lasted; but it seems too cruel that he should stay there now, cutting himself off from all the warmth and sweetness of the opening season. In vain I come to him with my hands full of dewy crocuses. In vain I hang about him, pleading for just a turn or two on the terrace where the sunshine falls hottest. He shakes his head, and is immoveable.

"No, petite," he says. "Not to-day."

"That is just what you said yesterday, Monsieur Maurice."

"And it is just what I shall say to-morrow, Gretchen, if you ask me again."

"But you won't stay in for ever, Monsieur Maurice!"

"Nay—'for ever' is a big word, little Gretchen."

"I don't believe you know how brightly the sun is shining!" I say coaxingly. "Just come to the window, and see."

Unwillingly enough, he lets himself be dragged across the room—unwillingly he looks out upon the glittering slopes and budding avenues beyond.

"Yes, yes—I see it," he replies with an impatient sigh; "but the shadow of that fellow in the corridor would hide the brightest sun that ever shone! I am not a galley-slave, that I should walk about with a garde-chiourme behind me."

"What do you mean, Monsieur Maurice?" I ask, startled by his unusual vehemence.

"I mean that I go free, petite—or not at all."

"Then—then you will fall ill!" I falter, amid fast-gathering tears.

"No, no—not I, Gretchen. What can have put that idea into your wise little head?"

"It was papa, Monsieur Maurice … he said you were"….

Then, thinking suddenly how pale and wasted he had become of late, I hesitated.

"He said I was—What?"

"I—I don't like to tell!"

"But if I insist on being told? Come, Gretchen, I must know what Colonel
Bernhard said."

"He said it was wrong to stay in like this week after week, and month after month. He—he said you were killing yourself by inches, Monsieur Maurice."

Monsieur Maurice laughed a short bitter laugh.

"Killing myself!" he repeated. "Well, I hope not; for weary as I am of it, I would sooner go on bearing the burden of life than do my enemies the favour of dying out of their way."

The words, the look, the accent made me tremble. I never forgot them.

How could I forget that Monsieur Maurice had enemies—
enemies who longed for his death?

So the first blush of early Spring went by; and the crocuses lived
their little life and passed away, and the primroses came in their
turn, yellowing every shady nook in the scented woods; and the
larches put on their crimson tassels, and the laburnum its mantle of
golden fringe, and the almond-tree burst into a leafless bloom of
pink—and still Monsieur Maurice, adhering to his resolve, refused
to stir one step beyond the threshold of his rooms.

Sad and monotonous now to the last degree, his life dragged
heavily on. He wrote no more. He read, or seemed to read, nearly
the whole day through; but I often observed that his eyes ceased
travelling along the lines, and that sometimes, for an hour and more
together, he never turned a page.

"My little Gretchen," he said to me one day, "you are too much in
these close rooms with me, and too little in the open air and sunshine."

"I had rather be here, Monsieur Maurice," I replied.

"But it is not good for you. You are losing all your roses."

"I don't think it is good for me to be out when you are always in-
doors," I said, simply. "I don't care to run about, and—and I don't
enjoy it."

He looked at me—opened his lips as if about to speak—then
checked himself; walked to the window; and looked out silently.

The next morning, as soon as I made my appearance, he said:—

"The French lesson can wait awhile, petite. Shall we go out for a
walk instead?"

I clapped my hands for joy.

"Oh, Monsieur Maurice!" I cried, "are you in earnest?"

For in truth it seemed almost too good to be true. But Monsieur
Maurice was in earnest, and we went—closely followed by the sentry.

It was a beautiful, sunny April day. We went down the terraces and slopes; and in and out of the flower-beds, now gaudy with Spring flowers; and on to the great central point whence the three avenues diverged. Here we rested on a bench under a lime-tree, not far from the huge stone basin where the fountain played every Sunday throughout the Summer, and the sleepy water-lilies rocked to and fro in the sunshine.

All was very quiet. A gardener went by now and then, with his wheelbarrow, or a gamekeeper followed by his dogs; a blackbird whistled low in the bushes; a cow-bell tinkled in the far distance; the wood-pigeons murmured softly in the plantations. Other passers-by, other sounds there were none—save when a noisy party of flaxen-haired, bare-footed children came whooping and racing along, but turned suddenly shy and silent at sight of Monsieur Maurice sitting under the lime-tree.

The sentry, meanwhile, took up his position against the pedestal of a mutilated statue close by, and leaned upon his musket.

Monsieur Maurice was at first very silent. Once or twice he closed his eyes, as if listening to the gentle sounds upon the air—once or twice he cast an uneasy glance in the direction of the sentry; but for a long time he scarcely moved or spoke.

At length, as if following up a train of previous thought, he said suddenly:—

"There is no liberty. There are comparative degrees of captivity, and comparative degrees of slavery; but of liberty, our social system knows nothing but the name. That sentry, if you asked him, would tell you that he is free. He pities me, perhaps, for being a prisoner. Yet he is even less free than myself. He is the slave of discipline. He must walk, hold up his head, wear his hair, dress, eat, and sleep according to the will of his superiors. If he disobeys, he is flogged. If he runs away, he is shot. At the present moment, he dares not lose sight of me for his life. I have done him no wrong; yet if I try to escape, it is his duty to shoot me. What is there in my captivity to equal the slavery of his condition? I cannot, it is true, go where I please; but, at least, I am not obliged to walk up and down a certain corridor, or in front of a certain sentry-box, for so many hours a day;

and no power on earth could compel me to kill an innocent man who had never harmed me in his life."

In an instant I had the whole scene before my eyes — Monsieur Maurice flying — pursued — shot down — brought back to die!

"But — but you won't try to run away, Monsieur Maurice!" I cried, terrified at the picture my own fancy had drawn.

He darted a scrutinising glance at me, and said, after a moment's hesitation: —

"If I intended to do so, petite, I should hardly tell Colonel Bernhard's little daughter beforehand. Besides, why should I care now for liberty? What should I do with it? Have I not lost all that made it worth possessing — the Hero I worshipped, the Cause I honoured, the home I loved, the woman I adored? What better place for me than a prison … unless the grave?"

He roused himself. He had been thinking aloud, unconscious of my presence; but seeing my startled eyes fixed full upon his face, he smiled, and said with a sudden change of voice and manner: —

"Go pluck me that namesake of yours over yonder — the big white Marguerite on the edge of the grass plat. Thanks, petite. Now I'll be sworn you guess what I am going to do with it! No? Well, I am going to question these little sibylline leaves, and make the Marguerite tell me whether I am destined to a prison all the days of my life. What! you never heard of the old flower sortilége? Why, Gretchen, I thought every little German maiden learned it in the cradle with her mother tongue!"

"But how can the Marguerite answer you, Monsieur Maurice?" I exclaimed.

"You shall see — but I must tell you first that the flower is not used to pronounce upon such serious matters. She is the oracle of village lads and lasses — not of grave prisoners like myself."

And with this, half sadly, half playfully, he began stripping the leaves off one by one, and repeating over and over again: —

"Tell me, sweet Marguerite, shall I be free? Soon — in time — perhaps — never! Soon — in time — perhaps — never! Soon — in time — perhaps — "

It was the last leaf.

"Pshaw!" he said, tossing away the stalk with an impatient laugh. "You could have given me as good an answer as that, little Gretch-en. Let us go in."

8

It was about a week after this when I was startled out of my deepest midnight sleep by a rush of many feet, and a fierce and sudden knocking at my father's bed-room door—the door opposite my own.

I sat up, trembling. A bright blaze gleamed along the threshold, and high above the clamour of tongues outside, I recognised my father's voice, quick, sharp, imperative. Then a door was opened and banged. Then came the rush of feet again—then silence.

It was a strange, wild hubbub; and it had all come, and gone, and was over in less than a minute. But what was it?

Seeing that fiery line along the threshold, I had thought for a moment that the Château was on fire; but the light vanished with those who brought it, and all was darkness again.

"Bertha!" I cried tremulously. "Bertha!"

Now Bertha was my Rhenish hand-maiden, and she slept in a closet opening off my room; but Bertha was as deaf to my voice as one of the Seven Sleepers.

Suddenly a shrill trumpet-call rang out in the courtyard.

I sprang out of bed, flew to Bertha, and shook her with all my strength till she woke.

"Bertha! Bertha!" I cried. "Wake up—strike a light—dress me quickly! I must know what is the matter!"

In vain Bertha yawns, rubs her eyes, protests that I have had a bad dream, and that nothing is the matter. Get up she must; dress herself and me in the twinkling of an eye; and go upon whatsoever dance I choose to lead her.

My father is gone, and his door stands wide open. We turn to the stairs, and a cold wind rushes up in our faces. We go down, and find the side-door that leads to the courtyard unfastened and ajar. There is not a soul in the courtyard. There is not the faintest glimmer of light from the guard-house windows. The sentry who walks perpetually to and fro in front of the gate is not at his post; and the gate is wide open!

Even Bertha sees by this time that something strange is afoot, and stares at me with a face of foolish wonder.

"Ach, Herr Gott!" she cries, clapping her hands together, "what's that?"

It is very faint, very distant; but quite audible in the dead silence of the night. In an instant I know what it is that has happened!

"It is the report of a musket!" I exclaim, seizing her by the hand, and dragging her across the courtyard. "Quick! quick! Oh, Monsieur Maurice! Monsieur Maurice!"

The night is very dark. There is no moon, and the stars, glimmering through a veil of haze, give little light. But we run as recklessly as if it were bright day, past the barracks, past the parade-ground, and round to the great gates on the garden side of the Château. These, however, are closed, and the sentry, standing watchful and motionless, with his musket made ready, refuses to let us through.

In vain I remind him that I am privileged, and that none of these gates are ever closed against me. The man is inexorable.

"No, Fräulein Gretchen," he says, "I dare not. This is not a fit hour for you to be out. Pray go home."

"But Gaspar, good Gaspar," I plead, clinging to the gate with both hands, "tell me if he has escaped! Hark; oh, hark! there it is again!"

And another, and another shot rings through the still night-air.

The sentry almost stamps with impatience.

"Go home, dear little Fräulein! Go home at once," he says. "There is danger abroad to-night. I cannot leave my post, or I would take you home myself.... Holy Saint Christopher! they are coming this way! Go—go—what would his Excellency the Governor say, if he found you here?"

I see quick gleams of wandering lights among the trees—I hear a distant shout! Then, seized by a sudden panic, I turn and fly, with Bertha at my heels—fly back the way I came, never pausing till I find myself once more at the courtyard gate. Here—breathless, trembling, panting—I stop to listen and look back. All is silent;—as silent as before.

"But, liebe Gretchen," says Bertha, as breathless as myself, "what is to do to-night?"

There is a coming murmur on the air. There is a red glow reflected on the barrack windows ... they are coming! I turn suddenly cold and giddy.

"Hush, Bertha!" I whisper, "we must not stay here. Papa will be angry! Let us go up to the corridor window."

So we go back into the house, upstairs the way we came, and station ourselves at the corridor window, which looks into the courtyard.

Slowly the glow broadens; slowly the sound resolves itself into an irregular tramp of many feet and a murmur of many voices.

Then suddenly the courtyard is filled with soldiers and lighted torches, and ... and I clasp my hands over my eyes in an agony of terror, lest the picture I drew a few days since should be coming true.

"What do you see, Bertha?" I falter. "Do you—do you see Monsieur Maurice?"

"No, but I see Gottlieb Kolb, and Corporal Fritz, and ... yes—here is Monsieur Maurice between two soldiers, and his Excellency the Colonel walking beside them!"

I looked up, and my heart gave a leap of gladness. He was not dead—he was not even wounded! He had been pursued and captured; but at least he was safe!

They stopped just under the corridor window. The torchlight fell full upon their faces. Monsieur Maurice looked pale and composed; perhaps just a shade haughtier than usual. My father had his drawn sword in his hand.

"Corporal Fritz," he said, turning to a soldier near him, "conduct the prisoner to his room, and post two sentries at his door, and one under his windows." Then turning to Monsieur Maurice, "I thank God, Sir," he said gravely, "that you have not paid for your imprudence with your life. I have the honour to wish you good night."

Monsieur Maurice ceremoniously took off his hat.

"Good night, Colonel Bernhard," he said. "I beg you, however, to remember that I had withdrawn my parole."

"I remember it, Monsieur Maurice," replied my father, drawing himself up, and returning the salutation.

Monsieur Maurice then crossed the courtyard with his guards, and entered the Château by the door leading to the state apartments. My father, after standing for a moment as if lost in thought, turned away and went over to the guard-house.

The soldiers then dispersed, or gathered into little knots of twos and threes, and talked in low voices of the events of the night.

"Accomplices!" said one, just close against the window where Bertha and I still lingered. "Liebe Mutter! I'll take my oath he had one! Why, it was I who first caught sight of the prisoner gliding through the trees—I saw him as plainly as I see you now—I covered him with my musket—I wouldn't have given a copper pfennig for his life, when paff! at the very moment I pulled the trigger, out steps a fellow from behind my shoulder, knocks up my musket, and disappears like a flash of lightning—Heaven only knows where, for I never laid eyes on him again!"

"What was he like?" asks another soldier, incredulously.

"Like? How should I know? It was as dark as pitch. I just caught a glimpse of him in the flash of the powder—an ugly, brown-looking devil he seemed! but he was gone in a breath, and I had no time to look for him."

The soldiers round about burst out laughing.

"Hold, Karl!" says one, slapping him boisterously on the shoulder. "You are a good shot, but you missed aim for once. No need to conjure up a brown devil to account for that, old comrade!"

Karl, finding his story discredited, retorted angrily; and a quarrel was fast brewing, when the sergeant on guard came up and ordered the men to their several quarters.

"Holy Saint Bridget!" said Bertha, shivering, "how cold it is! and there, I declare, is the Convent clock striking half after one! Liebe Gretchen, you really must go to bed — what would your father say?"

So we both crept back to bed. Bertha was asleep again almost before she had laid her head upon her pillow; but I lay awake till dawn of day.

9

It was in my father's disposition to be both strict and indulgent — that is to say, as a father he was all tenderness, and as a soldier all discipline. His men both loved and feared him; but I, who never had cause to fear him in my life, loved him with all my heart, and never thought of him except as the fondest of parents. Chiefly, perhaps, for my sake, he had up to this time been extremely indulgent in all that regarded Monsieur Maurice. Now, however, he conceived that it was his duty to be indulgent no longer. He was responsible for the person of Monsieur Maurice, and Monsieur Maurice had attempted to escape; from this moment, therefore, Monsieur Maurice must be guarded, hedged in, isolated, like any other prisoner under similar circumstances — at all events until further instructions should arrive from Berlin. So my father, as it was his duty to do, wrote straightway to the Minister of War, doubled all previous precautions, and forbade me to go near the prisoner's rooms on any pretext whatever.

I neither coaxed nor pleaded. I had an instinctive feeling that the thing was inevitable, and that I had nothing to do but to suffer and obey. And I did suffer bitterly. Day after day, I hung about the terraces under his windows, watching for the glimpse that hardly ever came. Night after night I sobbed till I was tired, and fell asleep with his name upon my lips. It was a childish grief; but not therefore the less poignant. It was a childish love, too; necessarily transient and irrational, as such childish passions are; but not therefore the less real. The dull web of my later life has not been without its one golden thread of romance (alas! how long since tarnished!), but not even that dream has left a deeper scar upon my memory than did the hero-worship of my first youth. It was something more than love; it was adoration. To be with him was measureless content—to be banished from him was something akin to despair.

So Monsieur Maurice and his little Gretchen were parted. No more happy French lessons—no more walks—no more stories told by the firelight in the gloaming! All was over; all was blank. But for how long? Surely not for ever!

"Perhaps the king will think fit to hand him over to some other gaoler," said my father one day; "and, by Heaven! I'd thank him more heartily for that boon than for the order of the Red Eagle!"

My heart sank at the thought. Many and many a time had I pictured to myself what it would be if he were set at liberty, and with what mingled joy and grief I should bid him good-bye; but it had never occurred to me as a possibility that he might be transferred to another prison-house.

Thus a week—ten days—a fortnight went by, and still there came nothing from Berlin. I began to hope at last that nothing would come, and that matters would settle down in time, and be as they were before. But of such vain hopes I was speedily and roughly disabused; and in this wise.

It was a gloomy afternoon—one of those dun-coloured afternoons that seem all the more dismal for coming in the midst of Spring. I had been out of the way somewhere (wandering to and fro, I believe, like a dreary little ghost, among the grim galleries of the state apartments), and was going home at dusk to be in readiness for my father, who always came in after the afternoon parade. Coming up the passage out of which our rooms opened, I heard voices—my father's and another. Concluding that he had Corporal Fritz with him, I went in unhesitatingly. To my surprise, I found the lamp lighted, and a strange officer sitting face to face with my father at the table.

The stranger was in the act of speaking; my father listening, with a grave, intent look upon his face.

..."and if he had been shot, Colonel Bernhard, the State would have been well rid of a troublesome burden."

My father saw me in the doorway, put up his hand with a warning gesture, and said hastily: —

"You here, Gretchen! Go into the dining-room, my child, till I send for you."

The dining-room, as I have said elsewhere, opened out of the sitting-room which also served for my father's bureau. I had therefore to cross the room, and so caught a full view of the stranger's face. He was a sallow, dark man, with iron grey hair cut close to his head, a hard mouth, a cold grey eye, and a deep furrow between his brows. He wore a blue military frock buttoned to the chin; and a plain cocked hat lay beside his gloves upon the table.

I went into the dining-room and closed the door. It was half-door, half-window, the upper panels being made of ground glass, so as to let in a borrowed light; for the little room was at all times somewhat of the darkest. Such as it was, this borrowed light was now all I had; for the dining-room fire had gone out hours ago, and though there were candles on the chimney-piece, I had no means of lighting them. So I groped my way to the first chair I could find, and waited my father's summons.

"And if he had been shot, Colonel Bernhard, the State would have been well rid of a troublesome burden."

It was all I had heard; but it was enough to set me thinking. "If he had been shot".... If who had been shot? My fears answered that question but too readily. Who, then, was this new-comer? Was he from Berlin? And if from Berlin, what orders did he bring? A vague terror of coming evil fell upon me. I trembled—I held my breath. I tried to hear what was being said, but in vain. The voices in the next room went on in a low incessant murmur; but of that murmur I could not distinguish a word.

Then the sounds swelled a little, as if the speakers were becoming more earnest. And then, forgetting all I had ever heard or been taught about the heinousness of eavesdropping, I got up very softly and crept close against the door.

"That is to say, you dislike the responsibility, Colonel Bernhard."

These were the first words I heard.

"I dislike the office," said my father, bluntly. "I'd almost as soon be a hangman as a gaoler."

The stranger here said something that my ear failed to catch. Then my father spoke again.

"To tell you the truth, Herr Count, I only wish it would please His Excellency to transfer him elsewhere."

The stranger paused a moment, and then said in a low but very distinct voice: —

"Supposing, Colonel Bernhard, that you were yourself transferred — shall we say to Königsberg? Would you prefer it to Brühl?"

"Königsberg!" exclaimed my father in a tone of profound amazement.

"The appointment, I believe, is worth six hundred thalers a year more than
Brühl," said the stranger.

"But it has never been offered to me," said my father, in his simple straightforward way. "Of course I should prefer it — but what of that? And what has Königsberg to do with Monsieur Maurice?"

"Ah, true — Monsieur Maurice! Well, to return then to Monsieur Maurice — how would it be, do you think, somewhat to relax the present vigilance?"

"To relax it?"

"To leave a door or a window unguarded now and then, for instance. In short, to—to provide certain facilities ... you understand?"

"Facilities?" exclaimed my father, incredulously. "Facilities for escape?"

"Well—yes; if you think fit to put it so plainly," replied the other, with a short little cough, followed by a snap like the opening and shutting of a snuff-box.

"But—but in the name of the Eleven Thousand Virgins, why wait for the man to run away? Why not give him his liberty, and get rid of him pleasantly?"

"Because—ahem!—because, you see, Colonel Bernhard, it would not then be possible to pursue him," said the stranger, drily.

"To pursue him?"

"Just so—and to shoot him."

I heard the sound of a chair pushed violently back; and my father's shadow, vague and menacing, started up with him, and fell across the door.

"What?" he shouted, in a terrible voice. "Are you taking me at my word? Are you offering me the hangman's office?"

Then, with a sudden change of tone and manner, he added:—

"But—I must have misunderstood you. It is impossible."

"We have both altogether misunderstood each other, Colonel Bernhard," said the stranger, stiffly. "I had supposed you would be willing to serve the State, even at the cost of some violence to your prejudices."

"Great God! then you did mean it!" said my father, with a strange horror in his voice.

"I meant—to serve the King. I also hoped to advance the interests of Colonel Bernhard," replied the other, haughtily.

"My sword is the King's—my blood is the King's, to the last drop," said my father in great agitation; "but my honour—my honour is my own!"

"Enough, Colonel Bernhard; enough. We will drop the subject."

And again I heard the little dry cough, and the snap of the snuff-box.

A long silence followed, my father walking to and fro with a quick, heavy step; the stranger, apparently, still sitting in his place at the table.

"Should you, on reflection, see cause to take a different view of your duty, Colonel Bernhard," he said at last, "you have but to say so before...."

"I can never take a different view of it, Herr Count!" interrupted my father, vehemently.

"—before I take my departure in the morning," continued the other, with studied composure; "in the meanwhile, be pleased to remember that you are answerable for the person of your prisoner. Either he must not escape, or he must not escape with life."

My father's shadow bent its head.

"And now, with your permission, I will go to my room."

My father rang the bell, and when Bertha came, bade her light the Count von
Rettel to his chamber.

Hearing them leave the room, I opened the door very softly and hesitatingly, scarce knowing whether to come out or not. I saw my father standing with his back towards me and his face still turned in the direction by which they had gone out. I saw him throw up his clenched hands, and shake them wildly above his head.

"And it was for this!—for this!" he said fiercely. "A bribe! God of Heaven! He offered me Königsberg as a bribe! Oh, that I should have lived to be treated as an assassin!"

His voice broke into hoarse sobs. He dropped into a chair—he covered his face with his hands.

He had forgotten that I was in the next room, and now I dared not remind him of my presence. His emotion terrified me. It was the first time I had seen a man shed tears; and this alone, let the man be whom he might, would have seemed terrible to me at any time. How much more terrible when those tears were tears of outraged honour, and when the man who shed them was my father!

I trembled from head to foot. I had an instinctive feeling that I ought not to look upon his agony. I shrank back — closed the door — held my breath, and waited.

Presently the sound of sobbing ceased. Then he sighed heavily twice or thrice — got up abruptly — threw a couple of logs on the fire, and left the room. The next moment I heard him unlock the door under the stairs, and go into the cellar. I seized the opportunity to escape, and stole up to my own room as rapidly and noiselessly as my trembling knees would carry me.

I had my supper with Bertha that evening, and the Count ate at my father's table; but I afterwards learned that, though the Governor of Brühl himself waited ceremoniously upon his guest and served him with his best, he neither broke bread nor drank wine with him.

I saw that unwelcome guest no more. I heard his voice under the window, and the clatter of his horse's hoofs as he rode away in the early morning; but that was long enough before Bertha came to call me.

10

Weeks went by. Spring warmed, and ripened, and blossomed into Summer. Gardens and terraces were ablaze once more with many-coloured flowers; fountains played and sparkled in the sunshine; and travellers bound for Cologne or Bonn put up again at Brühl in the midst of the day's journey, to bait their horses and see the Château on their way.

For in these years just following the Peace of Paris, the Continent was overrun by travellers, two thirds of whom were English. The diligence—the great, top-heavy, lumbering diligence of fifty years ago—used then to come lurching and thundering down the main street five times a week throughout the Summer season; and as many as three and four travelling carriages a day would pass through in fine weather. The landlord of the "Lion d'Or" kept fifty horses in his stables in those days, and drove a thriving trade.

So the Summer came, and brought the stir of outer life into the precincts of our sleepy Château; but brought no better change in the fortunes of Monsieur Maurice. Ever since that fatal night, the terms of his imprisonment had been more rigorous than ever. Till then, he might, if he would, walk twice a week in the grounds with a soldier at his heels; but now he was placed in strict confinement in his own two rooms, with one sentry always pacing the corridor outside his door, and another under his windows. And across each of those windows might now be seen a couple of bright new iron bars, thick as a man's wrist, forged and fixed there by the village blacksmith.

I have no words to tell how the sight of those bars revolted me. If instead of being a little helpless girl, I had been a man like my father, and a servant of the State, I think they would have made a rebel of me.

Worse, however, than iron bars, locked doors, and guarded corridors, was Hartmann—Herr Ludwig Hartmann, as he was styled in the despatch that announced his coming—a pale, slight, silent man, with colourless grey eyes and white eyelashes, who came direct from Berlin about a month later, to act as Monsieur Maurice's "personal attendant." Stealthy, watchful, secret, civil, he established himself in a room adjoining the prisoner's apartment, and was as much at home in the course of a couple of hours as if he had been settled there from the first.

He brought with him a paper of instructions, and, having on his arrival submitted these instructions to my father, he at once took up a certain routine of duties that never varied. He brushed Monsieur Maurice's clothes, waited upon him at table, attended him in his bed-room, was always within hearing, always on the alert, and haunted the prisoner like his shadow. Not even a housemaid could go in to sweep but he was present. Now the man's perpetual presence was intolerable to Monsieur Maurice. He had borne all else with patience, but this last tyranny was more than he could endure without murmuring. He appealed to my father; but my father, though Governor of Brühl, was powerless to help him. Hartmann had presented his instructions as a minister presents his credentials, and those instructions emanated from Berlin. So the new-comer, valet, gaoler, spy as he was, became an established fact, and was detested throughout the Château—by no one more heartily than myself.

I still, however, saw Monsieur Maurice now and then. My father often took me with him in his rounds, and always when he visited his prisoner. Sometimes, too, he would leave me for an hour with my friend, and call for me again on his way back; so that we were not wholly parted even now. But Hartmann took care never to leave us alone. Before my father's footsteps were out of hearing, he would be in the room; silent, unobtrusive, perfectly civil, but watchful as a lynx. We could not talk before him freely. Nothing was as it used to be. It was better than total banishments; it was better than never hearing his voice; but the constraint was hard to bear, and the pain of these meetings was almost greater than the pleasure.

And now, as I approach that part of my narrative which possesses the deepest interest for myself, I hesitate—hesitate and draw back before the great mystery in which it is involved. I ask myself what interpretation the world will put upon facts for which I can vouch; upon events which I myself witnessed? I cannot prove those events. They happened over fifty years ago; but they are as vividly present to my memory as if they had taken place yesterday. I can only relate them in their order, knowing them to be true, and leaving each reader to judge of them according to his convictions.

It was about the middle of the second week in June. Hartmann had been about six weeks at Brühl, and all was going on in the usual dull routine, when that routine was suddenly broken by the arrival of three mounted dragoons—an officer and two privates— whose errand, whatever it might be, had the effect of throwing the whole establishment into sudden and unwonted confusion.

I was out in the grounds when they arrived, and came back at midday to find no dinner on the table, no cook in the kitchen; but a full-dress parade going on in the courtyard, and all the interior of the Château in a state of wild commotion. Here were peasants bringing in wood, gardeners laden with vegetables and flowers, women running to and fro with baskets full of linen, and all to the accompaniment of such a hammering, bell-ringing, and clattering of tongues as I had never heard before.

I stood bewildered, not knowing what to do, or where to go.

"What is the matter? What has happened? What are you doing?" I asked, first of one and then of another; but they were all too busy to answer.

"Ach, lieber Gott!" said one, "I've no time for talking!"

"Don't ask me, little Fräulein," said another. "I have eight windows to clean up yonder, and only one pair of hands to do them with!"

"If you want to know what is to do," said a third impatiently, "you had better come and see."

The head-gardener's son came by with two pots of magnificent geraniums, one under each arm.

"Where are you going with those flowers, Wilhelm?" I asked, running after him.

"They are for the state salon, Fräulein Gretchen," he replied, and hurried on.

For the state salon! I ran round to the side of the grand entrance. There were soldiers putting up banners in the hall; others helping to carry furniture up stairs; carpenters with ladders; women with brooms and brushes; and Corporal Fritz bustling hither and thither, giving orders, and seeing after everything.

"But Corporal Fritz!" I exclaimed, "what are all these people about?"

"We are preparing the state apartments, dear little Fräulein," replied Corporal Fritz, rubbing his hands with an air of great enjoyment.

"But why? For whom?"

"For whom? Why, for the King, to be sure"; and Corporal Fritz clapped his hand to the side of his hat like a loyal soldier. "Don't you know, dear little Fräulein, that His Majesty sleeps here to-night, on his way to Ehrenbreitstein?"

This was news indeed! I ran up stairs—I was all excitement—I got in everybody's way—I tormented everybody with questions. I saw the table being laid in the grand salon where the King was to sup, and the bedstead being put up in the little salon where he was to sleep, and the ante-room being prepared for his officers. All was being made ready as rapidly, and decorated as tastefully, as the scanty resources of the Château would permit. I recognised much of the furniture from the attics above, and this, faded though it was, being helped out with flowers, flags, and greenery, made the great echoing rooms look gay and habitable.

By and by, my father came round to see how the work was going on, and finding me in the midst of it, took me by the hand and led me away.

"You are not wanted here, my little Gretchen," he said; "and, indeed, all the world is so busy to-day that I scarcely know what to do with thee."

"Take me to Monsieur Maurice!" I said, coaxingly.

"Ay—so I will," said my father; "with him, at all events, you will be out of the way."

So he took me round to Monsieur Maurice's rooms, and told me as we went along that the King had only given him six hours' notice, and that in order to furnish his Majesty's bed and his Majesty's supper, he had bought up all the poultry and eggs, and borrowed well-nigh all the silver, glass, and linen in the town.

By this time we were almost at Monsieur Maurice's door. A sudden thought flashed upon me. I pulled him back, out of the sentry's hearing.

"Oh, father!" I cried eagerly, "will you not ask the King to let Monsieur
eur

Maurice free?"

My father shook his head.

"Nay," he said, "I must not do that, my little Mädchen. And look you—not a word that the King is coming here to-night. It would only make the prisoner restless, and could avail nothing. Promise me to be silent."

So I promised, and he left me at the door without going in.

I spent all the afternoon with Monsieur Maurice. He divided his luncheon with me; he gave me a French lesson, he told me stories. I had not had such a happy day for months. Hartmann, it is true, was constantly in and out of the room, but even Hartmann was less in the way than usual. He seemed absent and preoccupied, and was therefore not so watchful as at other times. In the meanwhile I could still hear, though faintly, the noises in the rooms below; but all became quiet about five o'clock in the evening, and Monsieur Maurice, who had been told they were only cleaning the state apartments, asked no questions.

Meanwhile the afternoon waned, and the sun bent westward, and still no one came to fetch me away. My father knew where I was; Bertha was probably too busy to think about me; and I was only too glad to stay as long as Monsieur Maurice was willing to keep me. By and by, about half-past six o'clock, the sky became overclouded, and we heard a low muttering of very distant thunder. At seven, it rained heavily.

Now it was Monsieur Maurice's custom to dine late, and ours to dine early; but then, as his luncheon hour corresponded with our dinner-hour, and his dinner fell only a little later than our supper, it came to much the same thing, and did not therefore seem strange. So it happened that just as the storm came up, Hartmann began to prepare the table. Then, in the midst of the rain and the wind, my quick ear caught a sound of drums and bugles, and I knew the King was come. Monsieur Maurice evidently heard nothing; but I could see by Hartmann's face (he was laying the cloth and making a noise with the glasses) that he knew all, and was listening.

After this I heard no more. The wind raved; the rain pattered; the gloom thickened; and at half-past seven, when the soup was brought to table, it was so dark that Monsieur Maurice called for lights. He would not, however, allow the curtains to be drawn. He liked, he said, to sit and watch the storm.

A cover was laid for me at his right hand; but my supper hour was past, and what with the storm without, the heaviness in the air, and the excitement of the day, I was no longer hungry. So, having eaten a little soup and sipped some wine from Monsieur Maurice's glass, I went and curled myself up in an easy chair close to the window, and watched the driving mists as they swept across the park, and the tossing of the treetops against the sky.

It was a wild evening, lit by lurid gleams and openings in the clouds; and it seemed all the wilder by contrast with the quiet room and the dim radiance of the wax lights on the table. There was a soft halo round each little flame, and a dreamy haze in the atmosphere, from the midst of which Monsieur Maurice's pale face stood out against the shadowy background, like a head in a Dutch painting.

We were both very silent; partly because Hartmann was waiting, and partly, perhaps, because we had been talking all the afternoon. Monsieur Maurice ate slowly, and there were long intervals between the courses, during which he leaned his elbow on the table and his chin on his hand, looking across towards the window and the storm. Hartmann, meanwhile, seemed to be always listening. I could see that he was holding his breath, and trying to catch every faint echo from below.

It was a long, long dinner, and probably seemed all the longer to me because I did not partake of it. As for Monsieur Maurice, he tasted some dishes, and sent more away untouched.

"I think it is getting lighter," he said by and by. "Does it still rain?"

"Yes," I replied; "it is coming down steadily."

"We must open the window presently," he said. "I love the fresh smell that comes with the rain."

Here the conversation dropped again, and Hartmann, having been gone for a moment, came back with a dish of stewed fruit.

Then, for the first time, I observed there was a second attendant in the room.

"Will you not have some raspberries, Gretchen?" said Monsieur Maurice.

I shook my head. I was too much startled by the sight of the strange man, to answer him in words.

Who could he be? Where had he come from? He was standing behind Monsieur Maurice, far back in the gloom, near the door—a small, dark man, apparently; but so placed with regard to the table and the lights, that it was impossible to make out his features with distinctness.

Monsieur Maurice just tasted the raspberries and sent his plate away.

"How heavy the air of the room is!" he said. "Give me some Seltzer-water, and open that farthest window."

Hartmann reversed the order. He opened the window first; and as he did so, I saw that his hand shook upon the hasp, and that his face was deadly pale.

He then turned to the sideboard and opened a stone bottle that had been standing there since the beginning of dinner. He filled a tumbler with the sparkling water.

At the moment when he placed this tumbler on the salver—at the moment when he handed it to Monsieur Maurice—the other man glided quickly forward. I saw his bright eyes and his brown face in the full light. I saw *two hands* put out to take the glass; a brown hand and a white—his hand, and the hand of Monsieur Maurice. I saw— yes, before Heaven! as I live to remember and record it, I saw the brown hand grasp the tumbler and dash it to the ground!

"Pshaw!" said Monsieur Maurice, brushing the Seltzer-water impatiently from his sleeve, "how came you to upset it?"

But Hartmann, livid and trembling, stood speechless, staring at the door.

"It was the other man!" said I, starting up with a strange kind of breathless terror upon me. "He threw it on the ground—I saw him do it—where is he gone? what has become of him?"

"The other man! What other man?" said Monsieur Maurice. "My little
Gretchen, you are dreaming."

"No, no, I am not dreaming. There was another man—a brown man! Hartmann saw him—"

"A brown man!" echoed Monsieur Maurice. Then catching sight of Hartmann's face, he pushed his chair back, looked at him steadily and sternly; and said, with a sudden change of voice and manner:—

"There is something wrong here. What does it mean? You saw a man—both of you? What was he like?"

"A brown man," I said again. "A brown man with bright eyes."

"And you?" said Monsieur Maurice, turning to Hartmann.

"I—I thought I saw something," stammered the attendant, with a violent effort at composure. "But it was nothing."

Monsieur Maurice looked at him as if he would look him through; got up, still looking at him; went to the sideboard, and, still looking at him, filled another tumbler with Seltzer-water.

"Drink that," he said, very quietly.

The man's lips moved, but he uttered never a word.

"Drink that," said Monsieur Maurice for the second time, and more sternly.

But Hartmann, instead of drinking it, instead of answering, threw up his hands in a wild way, and rushed out of the room.

Monsieur Maurice stood for a moment absorbed in thought; then wrote some words upon a card, and gave the card into my hand.

"For thy father, little one," he said. "Give it to no one but himself, and give it to him the first moment thou seest him. There's matter of life and death in it."

11

How the King supped, how the King slept, and what he thought of his Château of Augustenburg which he now saw for the first time, are matters respecting which I have no information. I only know that I had fallen asleep on Monsieur Maurice's sofa when Bertha came at ten o'clock that night to fetch me home; that I was very drowsy and unwilling to be moved; and that I woke in the morning dreaming of a brown man with bright eyes, and calling upon Monsieur Maurice to make haste and come before he should again have time to vanish away.

It was a lovely morning; bright and fresh, and sunshiny after the night's storm. My first thought was of Monsieur Maurice, and the card he had entrusted to my keeping. I had it still. My father was not at home when I came back last night. He was in attendance on the King, and did not return till long after I was asleep in my own little bed. This morning, early as I awoke, he was gone again, on the same duty.

I jumped up. I bade Bertha dress me quickly. "I must go to papa," I said.
"I have a card for him from Monsieur Maurice."

"Nay, liebe Gretchen," said Bertha, "he is with the King."

But I told myself that I would find him, and see him, and give the card into his own hands, though a dozen kings were in the way. I could not read what was written on the card. I could read print easily and rapidly, but handwriting not at all. I knew, however, that it was urgent. Had he not said that it was matter of life or death?

I hurried to dress; I hurried to get out. I could not rest, I could not eat till I had given up the card. As good fortune would have it, the first person I met was Corporal Fritz. I asked him where I could find my father.

"Dear little Fräulein," said Corporal Fritz, "you cannot see him just yet.

He is with the King."

"But I must see him," I said. "I must—indeed, I must. Go to him for me—please go to him, dear, good Corporal Fritz, and tell him his little Gretchen must speak to him, if only for one moment!"

"But dear little Fräulein"....

"Is the King at breakfast?" I interrupted.

"At breakfast! Eh, then, our gallant King hath a soldier's habits. His Majesty breakfasted at six this morning, and is gone out betimes to visit his hunting-lodge at Falkenlust."

"And my father?"

"His Excellency the Governor is in attendance upon the King."

"Then I will go to Falkenlust."

Corporal Fritz shook his head; shrugged his shoulders; took a pinch of snuff.

"'Tis a long road to Falkenlust, dear little Fräulein," said he; "and His Excellency, methinks, would be better pleased"....

I stayed to hear no more, but ran off at full speed down the terraces, straight to the Round Point and the fountain, and along the great avenue that led to Falkenlust. I ran till I was out of breath—then rested—then ran again, on, and on, and on, till the road lengthened and narrowed behind me, and the Château of Augustenburg looked almost as small in the distance at one end as the Falkenlust Lodge at the other.

Then all at once, far, far away, I saw a moving group of figures. They grew larger and more distinct—they were coming towards me! I had run till I could run no farther. Panting and breathless, I leaned against a tree, and waited.

And now, as they drew nearer, I saw that the group consisted of some eight or ten officers, two of whom were walking somewhat in advance of the rest. One of the two wore a plain cocked hat and an undress military frock; the other was in full uniform, and wore two or three glittering medals on his breast. This other was my father. I scarcely looked at the first. I never even asked myself whether he was, or was not the King. I had no eyes, no thought for any but my father.

So I stood, eager and breathless, on the verge of the gravel. So they every moment drew nearer the spot where I was standing. As they came close, my father's eyes met mine. He shook his head, and frowned. He thought I had come there to stare at the King.

Nothing daunted, I took two steps forward. I had Monsieur Maurice's card in my hand. I held it out to him.

"Read it," I said. "It is from Monsieur Maurice."

But he crushed it in his hand without looking at it, and waved me back authoritatively.

"At once!" I cried; "at once!"

The gentleman in the blue frock stopped and smiled.

"Is this your little girl, Colonel Bernhard?" he asked.

My father replied by a low bow.

The strange gentleman beckoned me to draw nearer.

"A golden-haired little Mädchen!" said he. "Come hither, pretty one, and tell me your name."

I knew then that he was the King. I trembled and blushed.

"My name is Gretchen," I said.

"And you have brought a letter for your father?"

"It is not a letter," I said. "It is a card. It is from Monsieur Maurice."

"And who is Monsieur Maurice?" asked the King.

"So please your Majesty," said my father, answering the question for me,
"Monsieur Maurice is the prisoner I hold in charge."

The smile went out of the King's face.

"The prisoner!" he repeated, inquiringly. "What prisoner?"

"The state-prisoner whom I received, according to your Majesty's command, eight months ago—Monsieur Maurice."

"Monsieur Maurice!" echoed the King.

"I know the gentleman by no other name, please your Majesty," said my father.

The King looked grave.

"I never heard of Monsieur Maurice," he said, "I know of no state-prisoner here."

"The prisoner was consigned to my keeping by your Majesty's Minister of
War," said my father.

"By von Bulow?"

My father bowed.

"Upon whose authority?"

"In your Majesty's name."

The King frowned.

"What papers did you receive with your prisoner, Colonel Bernhard?" he said.

"None, your Majesty—except a despatch from your Majesty's Minister of War, delivered a day or two before the prisoner arrived at Brühl."

"How did he come? and where did he come from?"

"He came in a close carriage, your Majesty, attended by two officers who left Brühl the same night and whose names and persons are unknown to me. I do not know where he came from. I only know that they had taken the last relay of horses from Cologne."

"You were not told his offence?"

"I was told nothing, your Majesty, except that Monsieur Maurice was an enemy to the state, and—"

"And what?"

My father's hand went up to his moustache, as it was wont to do in perplexity.

"I — so please your Majesty, I think there is some foul mystery in it at bottom," he said, bluntly. "There hath been that thing proposed to me that I am ashamed to repeat. I do beseech your Majesty that some investigation…."

His eyes happened for a moment to rest upon the card. He stammered — changed colour — stopped short in his sentence — took off his hat — laid the card upon it — and so handed it to the King.

His Majesty Frederick William the Third of Prussia was, like most of the princes of his house, tanned, soldierly, and fresh-complexioned; but florid as he was, there came a darker flush into his face as he read what Monsieur Maurice had written.

"An attempt upon his life!" he exclaimed. "The thing is not possible."

My father was silent. The king looked at him keenly.

"*Is* it possible, Colonel Bernhard?" he said.

"I think it may be possible, your Majesty," replied my father in a low voice.

The King frowned.

"Colonel Bernhard," he said, "how can that be? You are responsible for the safety as well as the person of any prisoner committed to your charge."

"So long as the prisoner is left wholly to my charge I can answer for his safety with my head, so please your Majesty," said my father, reddening; "but not when he is provided with a special attendant over whom I have no control."

"What special attendant? Where did he come from? Who sent him?"

"I believe he came from Berlin, your Majesty. He was sent by your Majesty's
Minister of War. His name is Hartmann."

The King stood thinking. His officers had fallen out of earshot, and were talking together in a little knot some four yards behind. I was still standing on the spot to which the King had called me. He looked round, and saw my anxious face.

"What, still there, little one?" he said. "You have not heard what we were saying?"

"Yes," I said; "I heard it."

"The child may have heard, your Majesty," interposed my father, hastily; "but she did not understand. Run home, Gretchen. Make thy obeisance to his Majesty, and run home quickly."

But I had understood every word. I knew that Monsieur Maurice's life had been in danger. I knew the King was all-powerful. Terrified at my own boldness—terrified at the thought of my father's anger— trembling—sobbing—scarcely conscious of what I was saying, I fell at the King's feet, and cried:—

"Save him—save him, Sire! Don't let them kill poor Monsieur Maurice!
Forgive him—please forgive him, and let him go home again!"

My father seized me by the hand, forced me to rise, and dragged me back more roughly than he had ever touched me in his life.

"I beseech your Majesty's pardon for the child," he said. "She knows no better."

But the King smiled, and called me back to him.

"Nay, nay," he said, laying his hand upon my head, "do not be vexed with her. So, little one, you and Monsieur Maurice are friends?"

I nodded; for I was still crying, and too frightened at what I had done to be able to speak.

"And you love him dearly?"

"Better than anyone—in the world—except Papa," I faltered, through my tears.

"Not better than your brothers and sisters?"

"I have no brothers and sisters," I replied, my courage coming back again
by degrees. "I have no one but Papa, and Monsieur Maurice, and Aunt Martha
Baur—and I love Monsieur Maurice a thousand, thousand times more than Aunt
Martha Baur!"

There came a merry sparkle into the King's eyes, and my father turned his face away to conceal a smile.

"But if Monsieur Maurice was free, he would go away and you would never see him again. What would you do then?"

"I—should be very sorry," I faltered; "but"....

"But what?"

"I would rather he went away, and was happy."

The King stooped down and kissed me on the brow.

"That, my little Mädchen, is the answer of a true friend," he said, gravely and kindly. "If your Monsieur Maurice deserves to go free, he shall have his liberty. You have our royal word for it. Colonel Bernhard, we will investigate this matter without the delay of an hour."

Saying thus, he turned from me to my father, and, followed by his officers, passed on in the direction of the Château.

I stood there speechless, his gracious words yet ringing in my ears. He had left me no time for thanks, if even I could have framed any. But he had kissed me—he had promised me that Monsieur Maurice should go free, "if he deserved it!" and who better than I knew how impossible it was that he should not deserve it? It was all true. It was not a dream. I had the King's royal word for it.

I had the King's royal word for it—and yet I could hardly believe it!

12

I have told my story up to this point from my own personal experience, relating in their order, quite simply and faithfully, the things I myself heard and saw. I can do this, however, no longer. Respecting those matters that happened when I was not present, I can only repeat what was told me by others; and as regards certain foregone events in the life of Monsieur Maurice, I have but vague rumour; and still more vague conjecture upon which to base my conclusions.

The King had said that Monsieur Maurice's case should be investigated without the delay of an hour, and, so far as it could then and there be done, it was investigated immediately on his return to the Château. He first examined Baron von Bulow's original despatch, and all my father's minutes of matters relating to the prisoner, including a statement written immediately after the departure of a stranger calling himself the Count von Rettel, and detailing from memory, very circumstantially and fully, the substance of a certain conversation to which I had been accidentally a witness, and which I have myself recorded elsewhere.

The King, on reading this statement, was observed to be greatly disturbed. He questioned my father minutely as to the age, complexion, height, and general appearance of the said Count von Rettel, and with his own hand noted down my father's replies on the back of my father's manuscript. This done, His Majesty desired that the man Hartmann should be brought before him.

But Hartmann was nowhere to be found. His room was empty. His bed had not been slept in. He had disappeared, in short, as completely as if he had never dwelt within the precincts of the Château.

It was found, on more particular inquiry being made, that he had not been seen since the previous evening. Overwhelmed with terror, and perhaps with remorse, he had rushed out of Monsieur Maurice's presence, never to return. It was supposed that he had then immediately gathered together all that belonged to him, and had taken advantage of the bustle and confusion consequent on the King's arrival, to leave Brühl in one of the return carriages or fourgons that had brought the royal party from Cologne. I am not aware that anything more was ever seen or heard of him; or that any active search for him was judicially instituted either then, or at any other time. But he might easily have been pursued, and taken, and dealt with according to the law, without our being any the wiser at Brühl.

Hartmann being gone, the King then sent for the prisoner, and Monsieur Maurice, for the first time in many weeks, left his own rooms, and was brought round to the state-apartments. Seeing so many persons about; seeing also the flowers and flags upon the walls, he seemed surprised, but said nothing. Being brought into the royal presence, however, he appeared at once to recognise the King. He bowed profoundly, and a faint flush was seen to come into his face. He then cast a rapid glance round the room, as if to see who else was present; bowed also (but less profoundly) to my father, who was standing behind the King's chair; and waited to be spoken to.

"Vous êtes Français, Monsieur?" said the King, addressing him in French, of which language my father understood only a few words.

"Je suis Français, votre Majesté," replied Monsieur Maurice.

"Comment!" said the King, still in French. "Our person, then, is not unknown to you?"

"I have repeatedly enjoyed the honour of being in your Majesty's presence," replied Monsieur Maurice, respectfully.

Being then asked where, and on what occasion, my father understood him to say that he had seen his Majesty at Erfurt during the great meeting of the Sovereigns under Napoleon the First, and again at the Congress of Vienna; and also that he had, at that time, occupied some important office, such, perhaps, as military secretary, about the person of the Emperor. The King then proceeded to question him on matters relating to his imprisonment and his previous history, to all of which Monsieur Maurice seemed to reply at some length, and with great earnestness of manner. Of these explanations, however, my father's imperfect knowledge of the language enabled him to catch only a few words here and there.

Presently, in the midst of a somewhat lengthy statement, Monsieur Maurice pronounced the name of Baron von Bulow. Hereupon the King checked him by a gesture; desired all present to withdraw; caused the door to be closed; and carried on the rest of the examination in private. By and by, after the lapse of nearly three quarters of an hour, my father was recalled, and an officer in waiting was despatched to Monsieur Maurice's rooms to fetch what was left of the bottle of Seltzer-water, which Monsieur Maurice had himself locked up in the sideboard the night before.

The King then asked if there was any scientific man in Brühl capable of analysing the liquid; to which my father replied that no such person could be found nearer than Cologne or Bonn. Hereupon a dog was brought in from the stables, and, having been made to swallow about a quarter of a pint of the Seltzer-water, was presently taken with convulsions, and died on the spot.

The King then desired that the body of the dog, and all that yet remained in the bottle should be despatched to the Professor of Chemistry at Bonn, for immediate examination.

This done, he turned to Monsieur Maurice, and said in German, so that all present might hear and understand: —

"Monsieur, so far as we have the present means of judging, you have suffered an illegal and unjust imprisonment, and a base attempt has been made upon your life. You appear to be the victim of a foul conspiracy, and it will be our first care to sift that conspiracy to the bottom. In the meanwhile, we restore your liberty, requiring only your *parole d'honneur*, as a gentleman, a soldier, and a Frenchman, to present yourself at Berlin, if summoned, at any time required within the next three months."

Monsieur Maurice bowed, laid his hand upon his heart, and said: —

"I promise it, your Majesty, on my word of honour as a gentleman, a soldier, and a Frenchman."

"You are probably in need of present funds," the King then said; "and if so, our Secretary shall make you out an order on the Treasury for five hundred thalers."

"Believing myself to be beggared of all I once possessed, I gratefully accept your Majesty's bounty," replied Monsieur Maurice.

The King then held out his hand for Monsieur Maurice to kiss, which he did on bended knee, and so went out from the royal presence, a free man.

Half an hour later, he and I were strolling hand in hand under the trees. His step was slow, and the hand that held mine had grown sadly thin and transparent.

"Let us sit here awhile, and rest," he said, as we came to the bench by the fountain.

I reminded him that we had sat and rested in the same spot the very last time we walked together.

"Ay," he replied, with a sigh. "I was stronger then."

"You will get strong again, now that you are free," I said.

"Perhaps — if liberty, like most earthly blessings, has not come too late."

"Too late for what?"

"For enjoyment — for use — for everything. My friends believe me dead; my place in the life of the world is filled up; my very name is by this time forgotten. I am as one shipwrecked on the great ocean, and cast upon a foreign shore."

"Are you — are you going away soon?" I said, almost in a whisper.

"Yes," he said, "I go to-morrow."

"And you will — never — come back again?" I faltered.

"Heaven forbid!" he said quickly. Then, remembering how that answer would grieve me, he added; "but I will never forget thee, petite. Never, while I live."

"But — but if I never see you any more"....

Monsieur Maurice drew my head to his shoulder, and kissed my wet eyes.

"Tush! that cannot, shall not be," he said, caressingly. "Some day, perhaps, I may win back that old home by the sea of which I have so often told thee, little one; and then thou shalt come and visit me."

"Shall I?" I said, wistfully. "Shall I indeed?"

And he said—"Ay, indeed."

But I felt, somehow, that it would never come to pass.

After this, we got up and walked on again, very silently; he thinking of the new life before him; I, of the sorrow of parting. By-and-by, a sudden recollection flashed upon me.

"But, Monsieur Maurice," I exclaimed, "who was the brown man that stood behind your chair last night, and what has become of him?"

Monsieur Maurice turned his face away.

"My dear little Gretchen," he said, hastily, "there was no brown man. He existed in your imagination only."

"But I saw him!"

"You fancied you saw him. The room was dark. You were half asleep in the easy chair—half asleep, and half dreaming."

"But Hartmann saw him!"

"A wicked man fears his own shadow," said Monsieur Maurice, gravely. "Hartmann saw nothing but the reflection of his crime upon the mirror of his conscience."

I was silenced, but not convinced. Some minutes later, having thought it over, I returned to the charge.

"But, Monsieur Maurice," I said, "it is not the first time he has been here."

"Who? The King?"

"No—the brown man."

Monsieur Maurice frowned.

"Nay, nay," he said, impatiently, "prithee, no more of the brown man. 'Tis a folly, and I dislike it."

"But he was here in the park the night you tried to run away," I said, persistently. "He saved your life by knocking up the musket that was pointed at your head!"

Pale as he always was, Monsieur Maurice turned paler still at these words of mine. His very lips whitened.

"What is that you say?" he asked, stopping short and laying his hand upon my shoulder.

And then I repeated, word for word, all that I had heard the soldiers saying that night under the corridor window. When I had done, he took off his hat and stood for a moment as if in prayer, silent and bare-headed.

"If it be so," he said presently, "if such fidelity can indeed survive the grave—then not once, but thrice…. Who knows? Who can tell?"

He was speaking to himself. I heard the words, and I remembered them; but I did not understand them till long after.

The King left Brühl that same afternoon *en route* for Ehrenbreitstein, and Monsieur Maurice went away the next morning in a post-chaise and pair, bound for Paris. He gave me, for a farewell gift, his precious microscope and all his boxes of slides, and he parted from me with many kisses; but there was a smile on his face as he got into the carriage, and something of triumph in the very wave of his hand as he drove away.

Alas! how could it be otherwise? A prisoner freed, an exile returning to his country, how should he not be glad to go, even though one little heart should be left to ache or break in the land of the stranger?

I never saw him again; never—never—never. He wrote now and then to my father, but only for a time; perhaps as many as six letters during three or four years—and then we heard from him no more. To these letters he gave us no opportunity of replying, for they contained no address; and although we had reason to believe that he was a man of family and title, he never signed himself by any other name than that by which we had known him.

We did hear, however, (I forget now through what channel) of the sudden disgrace and banishment of His Majesty's Minister of War, the Baron von Bulow. Respecting the causes of his fall there were many vague and contradictory rumours. He had starved to death a prisoner of war and forced his widow into a marriage with himself. He had sold State secrets to the French. He had been over to Elba in disguise, and had there held treasonable intercourse with the exiled Emperor, before his return to France in 1815. He had attempted to murder, or caused to be murdered, the witnesses of his treachery. He had forged the King's signature. He had tampered with the King's servants. He had been guilty, in short, of every crime, social and political, that could be laid to the charge of a fallen favourite.

Knowing what we knew, it was not difficult to disentangle a thread of truth here and there, or to detect under the most extravagant of these fictions, a substratum of fact. Among other significant circumstances, my father, chancing one day to see a portrait of the late minister in a shop-window at Cologne, discovered that his former visitor, the Count von Rettel, and the Baron von Bulow were one and the same person. He then understood why the King had questioned him so minutely with regard to this man's appearance, and shuddered to think how deadly that enmity must have been which could bring him in person upon so infamous an errand.

And here all ended. The guilty and the innocent vanished alike from the scene, and we at least, in our remote home on the Rhenish border, heard of them no more.

Monsieur Maurice never knew that I had been in any way instrumental in bringing his case before the King. He took his freedom as the fulfillment of a right, and dreamed not that his little Gretchen had pleaded for him. But that he should know it, mattered not at all. He had his liberty, and was not that enough?

Enough for me, for I loved him. Ay, child as I was, I loved him; loved him deeply and passionately — to my cost — to my loss — to my sorrow. An old, old wound; but I shall carry the scar to my grave!

And the brown man?

Hush! a strange feeling of awe and wonder creeps upon me to this day, when I remember those bright eyes glowing through the dusk, and the swift hand that seized the poisoned draught and dashed it on the ground. What of that faithful Ali, who went forward to meet the danger alone, and was snatched away to die horribly in the jungle? I can but repeat his master's words. I can but ask myself "Does such fidelity indeed survive the grave? Who knows? Who can tell?"